HOME FOR THE HOLIDAYS

A NOVEL

GARY REILLY

Running Meter Press

DENVER

Published by
Running Meter Press
2509 Xanthia St.
Denver, CO 80238
Publisher@RunningMeterPress.com
720 328 5488
Cover art by John Sherffius

Composition by D. Kari Luraas
ISBN: 978-0-9847860-6-0

Library of Congress Control Number: 2013948346

First Edition 2013

Printed in the United States of America

Other Titles in The Asphalt Warrior Series

The Asphalt Warrior
Ticket to Hollywood
The Heart of Darkness Club

CHAPTER 1

I was sitting in Rocky Mountain Taxicab #123 outside the Brown Palace Hotel sipping a soda and eating a Twinkie when an elf climbed into my backseat. "Cherry Creek Shopping Center," he piped.

I put away my snacks, started the engine, dropped my red flag, and pulled out from the curb. This guy had appeared out of nowhere like elves always do, but he was dressed like a department store Santa Claus. I usually hate it when a pedestrian climbs into my taxi. A "pedestrian" is a person who doesn't come out of a hotel, who doesn't phone the cab company ahead of time for a ride, who comes off the sidewalk and hops into your cab and expects you to take him somewhere—which sounds logical, but it doesn't ameliorate the sense of gloom that engulfs a cabbie who is praying for a lucrative trip to Denver International Airport, only to see his hopes and dreams shattered by a legal technicality. To put it another way, a hotel cabstand is a designated zone on a city street set aside by the government for the special use of people like myself. Why I think I'm special is a separate issue, but thank God the city thinks so, too.

Fourth Santa this week. Two of them had gone to the Cherry Creek Shopping Center, but one of them—and get this—had gone to *Southglenn Mall!* What the Southglenn Santa was doing in downtown Denver when he was supposed to be dandling tots ten miles away I didn't know and I didn't ask. His nerves weren't up to it, I could tell. We both knew he was going to be late for his gig, but I didn't bring that up. Instead, I made a pretense at bravura taxi driving, which I have been good at for the past seven out of fourteen years of hacking the mean streets of Denver—not good at bravura driving, but pretending to be. This basically involves sudden starts at green lights and jarring stops at red lights. For some reason people think this gets them places faster. It's what I call an "illusion." Being a cab driver is not unlike being a magician—minus the top hat, the cape, the rabbit, and the gorgeous assistant. But you do have an audience.

In my case it's a mobile audience, which normally consists of one person. But an asphalt warrior's job is to put on a socko performance that inspires his audience to tip big.

It turned out the Southglenn Santa ended up ten minutes late for his gig because traffic was heavy that afternoon, but he was so grateful to me for bouncing him off the headliner that he gave me twenty bucks on a fourteen-dollar ride.

Just call me Merlin.

"Which department store?" I asked my Cherry Creek fare.

He knew what I was getting at. Part-time cab drivers and part-time Santas speak the same esperanto.

"Saks," he said. I could smell vodka on his breath. I glanced at my wristwatch. A quarter to one, meaning fifteen minutes until he went back onstage. I figured this without being told. I knew this guy was playing the clock like a quarterback, I could sense it. He stank of desperation. I didn't know what he was doing in downtown Denver and I wasn't about to ask. Maybe he had been at Sweeney's Tavern. Maybe there wasn't any place in Cherry Creek where a man who worked hard entertaining children could sneak a snort at noon. Maybe he didn't want to be spotted by the Cherry Creek authorities. Or maybe—just maybe—he had actual business downtown.

"What are you doing downtown on your lunch hour, if you don't mind my asking?" I said. My curiosity had gotten the best of me again. I have about as much willpower as a baby human.

"Payday," Santa said.

"If you don't mind my asking again, what kind of money can a guy make working as a Santa Claus?"

"Depends on how hard he's willing to work," the guy said.

I looked at him in my rearview mirror. I couldn't tell by his cherry red nose and the twinkle in his eye whether he was shucking or jiving me. "How hard can a Santa Claus possibly work?" I said.

"I could work every day if I wanted to," he said, "but I don't want to."

I liked that answer. I glanced at the mirror. "Let's say I worked every day from Thanksgiving through Christmas, how much money could I sock away?"

"Enough to pay for your stay at Bellevue."

I liked that even better.

"Are we talking five figures?" I said.

"Nah. Four figures tops. Maybe six grand. But that's if you work hard and steady. I'll come out of this season with three grand. More than enough to cover Christmas expenses."

"How did you get into this gig?" I said.

We were cruising down 1st Avenue by now. Cherry Creek was looming in the distance. I was trying to milk him for all the info I could gather. I thought I might try pretending to be jolly.

"A friend told me about it," he said. "That's how most of us get into it."

"Is there still time to apply?" I said.

"Nah. You gotta go down to the Santa agency in early November. There's training. You gotta do stuff."

My heart sank a couple inches. I lost interest in becoming jolly.

"Not everybody qualifies though," he said.

This caught my interest. I've never been "qualified" to do anything except sit and tap rubber-coated things with my toes. Some people call it "cab driving."

"What are the qualifications?" I said, but I no longer cared. Wave six grand under my nose and my brain goes right out the window. But it always comes home—just like Lassie, only sooner.

"A bushy white beard is the best qualification," he said. "If you have a real beard, you're automatically in."

"What if you don't have a beard?"

"Then you have to answer all kinds of questions."

Interesting concept. If I spent next year not shaving I would be exempt from a test. Why couldn't high school have been like that?

I pulled up in front of the door to Saks Fifth Avenue. Santa leaned forward and handed me a sawbuck and told me to keep the change. I suspected it was the vodka talking, but I didn't ask for a translation. When it comes to greenbacks, I'm as multilingual as the average non-American.

After Santa walked away, I debated whether to hang out at the mall or head back downtown. The Christmas shopping season had arrived and the mall was crawling with customers, which depressed me because it might cause me to decide to stay at the mall and work hard. But then Christmas always depresses me. In this way I think I am normal. Who doesn't get depressed during the holiday season? Who doesn't despair at the thought of making lots of money? It is virtually impossible for a cab driver to earn less than one hundred dollars a day during the Christmas shopping season. During Christmas, Americans go nuts trying to find somebody to take their money. It's the exact opposite of April 15th.

"Bah humbug," to quote a pro.

I decided to drift back downtown. I would be damned if I was going to get sucked into the mindless whirlpool of crass commercialism. I save that for novel writing.

"Four hundred east First Avenue," the dispatcher said, and my hand grabbed the mike before my brain got back from playing fetch with Timmy. I was driving past 400 East 1st right at that moment. See? This is what I hate about Christmas. It's magical.

"One twenty-three!" I barked. I always bark when I know other cabbies are grabbing their mikes. Newbies never stand a chance. It's the old pros I have to outdraw. I don't want to brag, but even Jack Palance couldn't outdraw Shane.

The fare was a young guy who had just undergone a tooth extraction at a dental office on 1st Avenue. I envied him. When I was in college I had a wisdom tooth pulled, and I was given a prescription for a bottle of narcotic pills that surely have reached the top of the DEA's hit-list by now. I don't remember the name of the pills, nor do I remember how I ended up in Tijuana. It's probably a long story.

"I need to go to Albertson's and have a prescription filled," the guy said. He looked to be around thirty. He was kind of woozy. The novocaine hadn't punched out for the day yet.

I drove him to the Albertson's at Alameda and Broadway.

"What kind of prescription pills are you getting?" I said. It was none of my business, but what's that got to do with my life?

"It's called Tylenol-B," he said.

My heart sank for him. It might as well have been aspirin, but I didn't say anything to the poor sap. I didn't tell him that there had once been a time in this country when prescriptions were written by doctors and not congressmen.

"Powerful drug," I said, hoping to cheer him up. I no longer envied his excruciating pain.

"Really?" he said.

"Tylenol-B?" I said. "I'm scared of that stuff."

His face lit up in my rearview mirror. I crossed my fingers and said a prayer to the patron saint of placebos. Call me a softie, but I knew the guy was doomed. The best he could hope for later on was a total absence of pain. Hell, I don't need drugs to reach that plateau. I own a 27-inch color TV.

I waited outside Albertson's while the guy went in to have his prescription filled. From where I sat I could see a store called SightCity!!! That was where I bought my first and last pair of glasses before converting to disposable contact lenses. I still have the glasses. In fact I have two for the price of one. I keep them in a chest of drawers, tucked in the rear next to an overdue library book. After I got the contact lenses I had the urge to throw the glasses away. It was an odd sort of urge, as though I had a craving to clear all the crap out of my life—but if I did that I wouldn't own anything.

The guy came out of Albertson's beaming with anticipation and clutching a little white package. He lived five blocks east of Broadway. I drove him there in silence. I felt guilty. I kept glancing at him in the rearview mirror. He was studying the writing on the package.

Tylenol-B.

Give me a break.

"Have a heavy trip, dude!" I chirped as he got out. He gave me ten bucks on a six-dollar ride. Now I really felt guilty. The word "oregano" kept welling up in my mind. Don't ask me why. I can't cook.

I headed back toward Lincoln Street. I listened to the Rocky radio just to hear the dispatcher hollering street numbers. Everybody in Denver wanted a taxi, but I gritted my teeth and set a course for true north, up Lincoln to 18th and over to the Brown Palace where I intended to wait for a trip to DIA even though nearby bells kept reaching out for me, east 17th, west 15th, Kinko's, the bus station, my God, it was like someone kicked a pop machine and cans were spilling onto the floor. That happened once when I was in the army. All us dogfaces got free sodas that night. The next morning the soda guy showed up and removed the pop machine from the dayroom permanently. End of parable.

There were six cabs in line at the Brown, so I moved on. I followed the road to the Fairmont, but there were seven cabs in line, so I moved on. When I got to the Hilton there were eight cabs parked at the curb, so I moved on. I felt like Country Charlie Rich. My elusive dream was doomed. It looked like I was going to be taking calls off the radio for the rest of the day.

I cursed the cabbies that were hogging the hotels—and I knew who they were, too. They were newbies. They were amateurs. They were *quitters!* They didn't have what it took to compete with the old pros by grabbing mikes and jumping bells, so they opted for the safety and security of the cabstands. I get thoroughly disgusted whenever I run into people just like me.

CHAPTER 2

"One twenty-three, one twenty-three, you've got a personal," the dispatcher said.

I was passing Union Station on my way to the Oxford Hotel to take a look at the cabstand. The Oxford was at the bottom of my list of potential hotels to hang around waiting for customers. During the previous fourteen years I had picked up exactly one fare at the Oxford—and guess what? He was going to Union Station, which is half a block away. He had a hell of a lot of nerve, as well as luggage. During the nineteenth century, the Oxford had been Denver's version of the Waldorf-Astoria, but times had changed. When I first arrived in Denver, the Oxford was a skid-row hotel. But thanks to urban redevelopment in Lower Downtown, financed by the Baby Boomers, the Oxford had gone from bust to boom again. I'm a Baby Boomer, but I wasn't part of the LoDo boom. I'm from the Bust Branch of the Boomers.

I like saying "LoDo boom," but I'll try not to say it again.

"One twenty-three," I said, picking up the mike. I was surprised to be told that I had a personal, since I hadn't arranged ahead of time to pick up any customers.

"Sweeney's," the dispatcher said. "The fare is inside."

My heart started to soar like an eagle. Sweeney's Tavern was my favorite watering hole, so hearing its name articulated over the radio was akin to hearing someone mention the title of a great movie that momentarily takes you back to the idyllic days of your youth, such as

the *Texas Chainsaw Massacre*. There's no denying the ineffable power
of poetry. But Sweeney's was also a place where drunks hung out, and
to be perfectly frank, I did not relish the idea of picking up a drunk.
This is the main reason I do not drive night shifts for Rocky Cab.
Last-call is the gold rush for night-shift drivers, but I have been to
the Yukon, and like Jack London, I won't be going back.

"Check," I said, and hung the mike on the dashboard. I was
three minutes away from Sweeney's Tavern. I hadn't been there for
awhile. Me and Sweeney were sort of on the outs because he had 86'd
me after I had been picked up by the police on suspicion of murder.
It was just a misunderstanding of course—I swear I never killed anybody. But it took forever to collect the proper paperwork necessary
to get Sweeney to rescind the 86. I'm talking police reports, character
witnesses, a letter from my Maw, the whole ball of wax. Trying to get
back into the good graces of a bartender is tougher than dealing with
the IRS. I finally decided it wasn't worth the effort.

But I did miss being in the joint and listening to the sound of
peanut shells crackling under my tennis shoes. It's the only bar I've
ever patronized in central downtown Denver, not counting emergen-
cies, so I really wanted things to get back to normal. But I was kind of
embarrassed to go in there. Word on the street said that Sweeney had
posted an article on the bulletin board clipped from the *Denver Post*
describing the details of my involvement in the kidnaping/murder,
which was not a kidnaping/murder at all but just one of those crazy
mix-ups. He had left it there because it's always a big deal when one
of the local "habitués" gets his name in the paper. "Habitués" is a
French word for "barflies." My Maw says "Eire" is the Gaelic word.

Yet there I was, aiming my radiator cap toward Sweeney's Tavern.
I didn't feel at all reluctant to go there, though, because I was working,
meaning this was a taxi call, a personal even, which gave me a good

excuse to walk in without feeling the least bit embarrassed, and it's rare that I get the opportunity to do things that don't embarrass me.

I parked in the no-parking zone right in front of Sweeney's door and climbed out. I stepped through the swinging doors and looked around.

"Top o' the morning to ye, Murph me boy!"

I froze.

I had forgotten that Harold was on duty during the daytime. I make a special point of forgetting Harold whenever I can. Harold is a young bartender. That's all I want to say about Harold, except that it was four in the afternoon.

"Rocky Cab!" I shouted. This was an acceptable formal protocol. You may have experienced this yourself. It's not uncommon for a taxi driver to enter a bar and announce his presence like a town crier. I get a kick out of doing it. It makes me feel like a raucous juvenile delinquent. I was hoping that my "personal," whoever he was, would hop off a barstool and follow me outside before Harold had a chance to talk again. But I've never had much luck with hope. I generally avoid it.

"Rocky Cab!" I shouted again. Harold came out from behind the bar. Happy Hour was still an hour away so there were practically no customers in the bar, but I took a deep breath in preparation for screaming at the top of my lungs for the third time anyway. Then Harold placed an index finger to my lips and said, "Shhh, you'll wake him."

Never in my wildest dreams had I ever thought my lips would be touched by any part of Harold's body. I snatched his wrist and said, "You better not be talking about my customer."

He nodded and pointed with his other hand toward the far corner of the tavern where the countertop makes an L and stops at the wall. Santa Claus was asleep on the baseline.

"What the hell *is* this, Harold?" I said, shoving his hand away.

"That man dressed in those bright red clothes asked me to call you. He needs a ride to work."

"Fer the luvva Christ," I mumbled, heading toward the corner. Which Santa was it? One of the Cherry Creek Santas, or the Southglenn Santa? I had my fingers crossed for Southglenn. Finger-crossing is as close as I ever get to hope, and about as effective.

Santa was face down on the bar. A group of shot glasses were arranged around his head like eight tiny reindeer.

"Jaysus, Harold," I said. "How could you let him drink eight shots of hard liquor while in uniform?"

"He kept paying me."

"And what are those glasses doing next to his head?" I said. "Didn't they teach you to remove shot glasses in bartending school?"

"I was absent that day."

"Listen up, Harold. When a customer is determined to drink himself to death, you do one of two things. You either refill the used shot glass with fresh liquor, or you put the used glass into the sink and fill a new glass with liquor. But you *never* leave the empties where his wife can count them."

"I'm sorry, Murph. I wasn't thinking."

"All right. Now. What's the story with this guy?"

"He says he knows you. He asked me to call you personally for a ride to his job."

"Did he say where he knows me from?"

"He told me he used to work with you."

"I want you to boil up a pot of coffee—black," I said to Harold.

I took hold of Santa's shoulders and raised him to an upright position. "Wake up, pal, it's time to go to work," I said, feeling like a traitor to the human race.

By the time Harold brought me a cup of steaming joe, the Santa was returning to consciousness. You know the drill. Fluttering eyelashes. Groans. Mumbles. Hacking cough. That was me. Santa merely opened his eyes and said, "Murph!"

I was still in the dark.

"Here, drink this," I said, taking the cup of mud and handing it to him.

He had trouble with the cup. He was blotto alright, but he knew who I was. I didn't know him though, and I was determined to get to the bottom of this mystery before Harold talked again.

"Murph … you showed up," Santa said.

"Who are you, and why did you call me?" I said.

"Don't you remember me, Murph?" he said. He pulled off his beard and red hat. "We used to work together."

"Where?" I said.

"Dyna-Plex."

My hair stood on end, and that's an impressive sight when you've got a ponytail. But that was all it took. I recognized the guy now. The years had not been kind to him from the neck up. He had been my supervisor back in the days when I wrote a monthly brochure for the Dyna-Plex Corporation down in the Denver Tech Center. His name was Carlton Giles. He was the guy I had resigned to. I had told him that I was going to work for Rocky Cab until something better came along. This turned out to be true.

"My God, Giles, what happened to you?" I said. "How in the hell did you become a Santa?"

"I was downsized," he mumbled.

"Are you supposed to be at a gig right now?"

He nodded. "Five o'clock."

"Jaysus, Giles, what are you doing drinking when you're supposed to be deceiving children?"

"Children," he said. "I wish."

"What do you mean?"

"I'm not a department-store Santa," he said. He could barely mouth his words. "I work the corporate circuit."

That was a new one on me. "What's that?"

"Office parties."

"Fer the luvva Christ," I said. "Finish that coffee. You've got forty-five minutes before you go onstage."

I turned and looked at Harold. "I'm going to need a cup of java to go."

The kid surprised me. Instead of wringing his hands and whining that fixing a cup of coffee to go was a hassle beyond the realm of human capability, he went right to work.

I dragged Giles off his stool, then herded him out the door and into the backseat of 123. When I turned around to go back inside the tavern, Harold was already outside with the cup of coffee in his hand.

"Thanks, kid," I said. It felt funny expressing gratitude to Harold. He had always been such a twit, and now he was acting like a pro. I finally had to admit to myself that my little Harold was growing up.

"Your friend didn't pay for his last drink," Harold said. "Plus the coffee."

"Put it on my tab," I said.

"Sweeney froze your tab after you killed that guy."

"I didn't *kill* the guy, Harold. You heard him on my answering machine, fer the luvva Christ."

"All I know is, your friend owes me four dollars," Harold said. I gave him the money out of my own pocket.

It was only after I pulled away from the curb that I realized I hadn't included a tip. This made me feel bad. Harold may have been Harold, but he was also a bartender. He deserved better. This was turning out to be the worst Christmas ever.

CHAPTER 3

"Where to?" I said.

"DynaPlex," Giles said.

I gritted my teeth. Now I understood why he had gotten drunk. "At least you're wearing a Santa costume," I said. "Nobody will recognize you. How long does your gig last?"

"An hour."

"Don't worry, you'll be okay. Also, you owe me four dollars for the drinks you didn't pay for."

He nodded again and took another sip of coffee.

We drove south in silence. Giles made a dent in his joe. A big dent. Big enough to pour a half-pint of vodka into the cup, which was exactly what he did. After I pulled up in front of Dyna-Plex, I turned around and saw him lying on the backseat with the half-pint in his hand. It was empty.

"Giles!" I hollered. "Get to work!"

"I can't do it, Murph," he said. "You gotta do it for me."

My ponytail went straight through the roof. I turned and looked up at the glass facade of Dyna-Plex. It had been fifteen years since I had walked out of that place and simultaneously quit smoking. I turned and looked at Giles's prone form. "How much do you get paid for this gig?"

"Hundred and a half," he mumbled.

"For an *hour's* work!" I choked.

He nodded and lost consciousness.

My world was shaken that day. I was in the wrong line of work altogether.

But Giles looked like he needed a hundred and a half, so I decided to help him. "Empathy" is one of the two job descriptions of being an asphalt warrior. The other is "drive safely."

Fortunately, Giles was wearing blue jeans and a T-shirt under his costume. I didn't want to leave a naked man lying in my backseat. But I did turn on the waiting-meter before I got out of the cab. This was legal, although it did violate the spirit of Christmas at the going rate of twenty cents a minute. I would be gone for only an hour though. You do the math.

The moment I stepped through the doors of Dyna-Plex it was as if I had entered a dream. I've had dreams about every place I've ever worked in my life. Sometimes I dream I'm back in the army and plenty annoyed about it. The strangest thing about the army dreams is that I grab a mop even though I know I had been discharged years ago. Why am I like that in my dreams? Why do I acquiesce so quickly? Why am I like that in real life?

The dream increased in intensity when I pressed the button for the sixth floor, which was where I had worked fifteen years earlier. The elevator door silently opened and a chill crept up my spine. What if Carlton Giles had actually been sent to bring me back to Dyna-Plex, like the Ghost of Christmas Past escorting Ebenezer Scrooge to Fezziwig's warehouse in order to teach him a valuable life lesson? The Santa suit, my former office, the convenient way I had bamboozled myself into doing him a favor. The whole scenario stank of personal growth.

But considering the fact that it had been fifteen years since I had worked at Dyna-Plex, I didn't know why I was so leery about going in there. Most of the people I had worked with would have retired, quit, or been downsized long ago, so you can imagine how peculiar I felt when I recognized every person who showed up at the Christmas party. I didn't see a missing face.

Linda was still seated behind the reception desk where she had been sitting when I walked out of Dyna-Plex fifteen years earlier.

I recalled that day. I had just lit my last cigarette ever, and was "shooting the bull" with her, as they say in the corporate world, before I said my goodbyes. I kind of had my eye on her back then, but I had never seen her stand up, so I wasn't entirely certain she had legs. But those were the days when I judged a woman based on her physical attributes. I have evolved as a male since then. I no longer value physical attributes. I would sell my own legs if I could and use the money to buy a 52-inch color TV.

"Oh good, you're here," she said to me for the first time in her life.

She stood up. I immediately started valuing attributes again. She had two legs—count 'em!—that led me down a hallway to a small room where I was handed a large bag filled with presents.

"I'll tell the boss you're here," she said with a smile that was so plastic, so shiny, and so beautiful that I almost asked for a job application. Never before had I encountered the kind of women employed at Dyna-Plex. I was so mesmerized by the perfection of their hair-do's, foreheads, face powder, eyeliner, noses, ears, cheeks, lipstick, teeth, chins, and everything from the neck down, that I used to secretly stare at the women as they walked past my desk, and I am not referring to "lust" at this particular moment, although I might swing by there in a minute.

I had a private office when I worked at Dyna-Plex. It was just a small room, but it beat a cubicle. The top brass at Dyna-Plex seemed to think that in-house writers needed privacy in order to "focus on a vision of corporate goals." I put that in quotes because I wrote that phrase sixteen years ago when I submitted a request for a private office.

When I was first hired, I was given a desk in "the big room" as we called it, a large room filled with dozens of desks where the typing-pool secretaries and low-level male employees worked. By "low-level" I mean me. But I convinced the top brass that I needed to be put into a room out of sight of the rest of the office. I think they wanted the big room to be used only by people who could type with more than one finger.

"Ho ho ho!" I barked as I walked in. It was like being in Sweeney's again. Twice in one day I had found myself hollering at the top of my lungs in a place of business, and I was starting to like it. This did not bode well, since practically everything I like has gotten me into "fixes" at one time or another, with the exception of television watching. I can't think of a single instance where TV has affected my life in a negative way, not counting a ThighMaster, but let's not get into that.

Just before I sat down on a big chair that had been set up for the Santa, I glanced at my wristwatch. Only fifty-nine minutes to go. I might not have made it through that hour, but as I often say, being a cab driver is a lot like being an actor. You could be the most reclusive curmudgeon on the planet, but when you turn on your meter and say "Where to?" it's like the curtain has risen on a Broadway musical—suddenly you're Ethel Merman.

"Merry Christmas everybody!" I boomed.

The employees formed a standing circle around me, some of them holding mixed drinks. It was odd having all these familiar face-less entities staring at me. I felt sneaky.

During the ritual of handing out small packages, I was offered a cup of spiked Kool-Aid—purple I might add. "I never drink and fly," I said, and they actually laughed. Suddenly I understood television.

I read each name aloud as I handed out packages, which contained gold-plated pen-and-pencil sets and staplers with names engraved on them, stuff like that. It was chummy. But it gave me the creeps to say, "Dale ... Connie ... Barb ... Kip ..." since I deliberately had never learned any of their names when I worked there. Long before I had gotten the job at Dyna-Plex, I had discovered that once you learn a person's name, sooner or later he will say, "Hi."

After the gifts were handed out, I glanced at my watch. Twenty minutes to go, although I assumed the gig was over since the bag was empty. Then somebody brought out a goddamn Polaroid. That was "The Day Hell Came To Dyna-Plex." Only three of the male employees were drunk enough to sit on me, but every stenographer had to have her picture taken while nestled on Kris Kringle's lap.

At first it was funny. You can carve that on my tombstone. But after the tenth perfume-factory got comfy on my lap, I was starting to sweat. It was the most pointless experience of my life, if you get my drift. I had to get out of there. I glanced at my wristwatch overtly, hoping someone in charge would "get the message." But the top brass were paying the Santa agency a hundred and a half, and they expected a full hour of work in return. Republicans are like that. I didn't actually know the politics of anybody there, but I didn't see any hippies knocking back schnapps.

Then Carlton Giles walked in.

By "walked," I mean "crawled."

"Murph ... there you are," he gasped. The secretary screamed and jumped off my lap. I don't know if it was my name or the sight of Giles. You be the judge.

"You left your meter running," he said. "I thought you would want to know that." He was trying to be helpful, the most feared creature in the forest.

I stood up and said, "Ho ho ho!" and grabbed Giles by the arm, hoisted him to his feet, and escorted him out the door toward the bank of elevators. I began jabbing buttons even though I knew that one push was all you get.

As an aside, I do not believe that pedestrian-crosswalk buttons actually work. I don't know why I bring that up.

But back to the worst Christmas ever. I kept punching buttons and waiting for a Republican to come charging out of the big room. I once worked as a janitor in a printing plant, and the owner told me that Democrats never pay their bills. I don't know why I bring that up either.

The elevator door opened. I shoved Giles inside. I wasn't certain if we would beat "security" to the front door, but one thing I did know was "the secret of the elevator." If you don't know "the secret of the elevator," here it is. If you hold your finger against an elevator button, nine times out of ten it will bypass every floor where people are waiting, and take you directly to your floor. Keep that under your hat. I've probably broken a federal law just by mentioning it. And if I haven't, I'm sure somebody is getting busy writing one.

I hauled Giles outside and leaned him up against my cab, then opened the rear door. I picked him up like a pair of skis and slid him into the backseat.

"Where do you live?" I said.

By the time I had transferred him to the safe custody of the janitor of his apartment building, he was unconscious.

I don't know if Giles ever got his hundred and a half, or if he even made it through the holidays as a Santa, and I don't want to know. But this I do know: I never got paid for the Sweeney tab, the trip to DTC, or the waiting-time. Ergo, I had learned a valuable life lesson after all from my journey into the past: thanks to Giles, I now know why my friends never visit me anymore. I used to think it was because I asked them not to.

CHAPTER 4

"Can yeh make it home for Christmas, boy-o?"

It was the day after "The Giles Incident." A phone message was waiting in my apartment. Up until then I had gotten along well with my answering machine. It talked to me and I ignored it. I don't know why it's even called an "answering" machine.

It was a gift to me from a man for whom I had once done a favor, and I hung on to it even though I had mixed feelings about listening to people demanding that I acknowledge their existence. But the thing that tipped the scale in favor of keeping the machine was the fact that the people weren't present when they were making the demand, which was a new experience in my life. Prior to that, the only way to avoid acknowledging the existence of friends and strangers was to become a total recluse, which worked out fairly well, although it made shopping difficult.

I had pulled a twelve-hour shift that day, toted up twenty-eight rides, and earned a profit of one hundred and five dollars. I hadn't worked that hard by accident ever. It's true that I had earned more money when I was a newbie driver, but back then I did it on purpose. This was before I figured out the Work/Loaf Ratio for driving a hack.

I've never been good at mathematics, so it took me a couple of months of juggling the W/LR to lower my daily pay to a steady fifty bucks per shift. Believe me, it's a balancing act. You have to be able to calculate how many hours you can sit outside a hotel waiting for fares to come out the door, versus how many calls you have to take off the radio in order to maintain minimum profits. There were plenty of days when I botched the formula and went home with seventy bucks feeling like a failure.

When I got into my crow's nest that night I dropped my plastic briefcase on the kitchen table and trudged into the living room pulling the wad of dough out of my shirt pocket and looking at it with disgust. It served only to remind me of how hard I had worked. I won't bore you with the day's details, except to say that I had gotten caught up in a web of bells—meaning I had found myself wrestling with one of those intolerable situations that cab drivers occasionally experience. This involves picking up a new fare almost as soon as you drop off your last fare. Those five-dollar bills kept rolling in, and if the fare had gotten a jump on his Yuletide joy early, it sometimes came to ten dollars for a three-dollar trip. Need I say more?

Then I noticed the blinking red light on my answering machine. The red light hadn't bothered me when I first got the machine because it was a signal that another batch of optimists had called my apartment while I was out.

I pulled my copy of *Finnegans Wake* off the bookshelf and stuffed my profits for the day into it, then listened to my phone message.

"Can yeh make it home for Christmas, boy-o?"

It was me ol' Mither. I would recognize her voice almost anywhere. It nearly broke my heart because the call had been made in the afternoon, which meant she paid the highest long-distance charges between Wichita and Denver. I tried never to cost my Maw money, especially after she told me to stop doing it. And now here she was, asking me to do something I had never done before in my life, which was to come home for Christmas.

Most of the Christmases I had endured at home were the result of the fact that I lived there, so I had no way to escape. But after I dropped out of college and went out into the world I hadn't been back to Wichita, except for me ol' Dad's funeral eight years ago, but I don't count that as "going home." That's just something kids have to do. "Going home" on the other hand implies volition, and I haven't practiced that in years—forty-five to be exact.

"Can yeh make it home for Christmas, boy-o?"

I listened to the message one more time. She said a few other things, like "Hello?" with the standard lilt of a question mark, as well as, "I know yer there, so pick up." We hadn't communicated since I had gotten the answering machine, but this remark indicated that she had plenty of experience with other answering machines. There was an undercurrent of authority in her voice. My evil brother Gavin out in California owned an answering machine. I hadn't spoken to him in five years, not since my last trip through Reno, but my Maw filled in the gaps when she wrote letters to the siblings.

I really don't want to know what my brother and sisters are ever up to. Like myself, Gavin is unmarried, and like myself, he seems to be happy. He works in an office and makes lots of money. Or maybe he owns the business, I've never been clear on that. My three sisters, Mary, Sally, and Shannon Lucy are married and they, too, seem to be happy. But seeming to be happy is an Irish-Catholic trait and shouldn't be taken too seriously. For example, all through high school I seemed to be happy whenever a nun was in the immediate vicinity, but that was just a survival tactic—sort of like a frightened gazelle standing motionless while a panther strolled past.

I erased the message on the answering machine. I don't want to get too Freudian here, but it made me feel good to do that. Kind of like setting my wristwatch ahead ten minutes, which I used to do until I began driving a cab. It gave me a "safe" feeling to set my clocks ahead ten minutes in those days, as if I was surrounding myself with an impregnable bubble of Time that no one could penetrate in order to "get at" me. I started doing that after I went to work at Dyna-Plex.

To sum up the reason for this quirk, sitting at a desk all day made me want to crawl right out of my own skin. One afternoon about three weeks into the job I glanced at my wristwatch and saw that there were ten minutes left until quitting time. I felt like a heroin addict in the final throes of cold turkey. I was sweating like a madman. My teeth were chattering. Red ants were burrowing under my skin. A guy at the water cooler was talking about his golf grip. I began staring at the second-hand of my wristwatch trying to use telekinesis to make it speed up. That didn't work in high school either. But in high school I didn't have access to the clock above the blackboard. Suddenly I pulled out the stem on my wristwatch and moved the minute-hand ahead to five o'clock, and the result was like a mainline injection of the most feared and addictive controlled substance on the DEA's hit-list. A calm came over me. My flesh dried up and the red ants vanished. In my world it was five o'clock.

For the next year, I was ten minutes ahead of everyone else in the office. While they were frantically tearing their hair out trying to meet deadlines, I was watching from a detached distance, like James Joyce paring his fingernails. But I quit setting my watch ahead when I went to work for Rocky Cab. You have to know exactly what time it is when you drive a taxi. Sitting outside an apartment building and honking your horn for ten minutes not only diminishes the likelihood of getting a tip, it attracts cops.

After I erased Maw's message I went back into the kitchen and fried a burger, then carried it and a beer into the living room and sat down to eat dinner and watch *Gilligan's Island*. But I couldn't concentrate on the TV. It was one of the lesser *Gilligan's* anyway, if that's not an oxymoron. It was the episode where Mr. and Mrs. Howell split up and the other castaways try to get them back together. I didn't buy the premise for one second. Thurston Howell was loaded. What was Lovey going to do if she walked away from the Howell fortune—open a boutique? Ha! I'm sorry, Sherwood Schwartz, but you stretched my credulity to the breaking point on that one.

It didn't matter though. I kept thinking about the fact that I would have to call my Maw back. It's just something kids have to do.

I finally turned off the TV during the scene where the castaways "tricked" Thurston into sharing a candlelit dinner with Lovey. Who did Thurston think he was going to have dinner with anyway—Mary Ann? *My* Mary Ann? Over my dead body, copperboss.

I carried the dish into the kitchen, did it, then returned to the living room and sat down next to the telephone. I dialed up Wichita. I knew the number by heart. Maw made me memorize it before she kicked me out of the house twenty years ago.

"Maw?" I said. "It's me."

"Brendan?" she said. "Is that you?"

"It's me," I repeated. We go through this every time.

"An answering machine, eh?" she said. "Did yeh hit the lottery?"

"No, Maw."

"Did yeh come by it honestly?"

"Yes, Maw."

"Why do yeh need an answering machine anyway, Brendan? Are yeh trying to put on airs?"

"I gave up trying years ago, Maw."

"Yer brother has an answering machine too, yeh know."

"I know Maw. You wrote me about that."

"You and yer brother are just like yer Uncle Seamus," she said.

"He was the faarst in the family to own a television set, him and his lace-curtain wife."

While it might not appear so on the surface, this conversation was careening wildly out of control. I had to act fast.

"Are the others coming home for Christmas?" I said.

"Yer the last holdout," she said.

"Why the sudden invite, Maw? I haven't been home for Christmas in twenty years."

"Ah Brendan," she said with a sigh. "This may be the last Christmas that we can celebrate with the whole family together. Everyone has scattered to the winds, and it's getting difficult for the girls to talk their husbands into coming to Wichita. They have their own families now. But this year everyone is going to show up."

Then came "The Moment" as I call it—the moment in all phone conversations when a member of the family asks, "How are things going?" It's like being grilled by an investigative reporter. I never have anything to say because nothing in my life is ever going anywhere. But over the years I have learned how to finesse this intrusion into meaninglessness by relating a quick anecdote that is so banal that it kills the conversation. I told my Maw about my little adventure at Dyna-Plex playing Santa Claus for a man who was too drunk to ho ho. I left out the part about not getting paid. I didn't want to bore her. Most of my stories ended that way.

"I'll be home for Christmas, Maw."

"I always told the good sisters at Blessed Virgin that yeh were smarter than yeh looked, boy-o," she said. Then she said we better ring off before the high rates kicked in. The women of the Murphy family always had the heads for money. But then technically she wasn't really a Murphy. Me ol' Mither had been a Clancy in her youth. A Boston Clancy. Nuff said.

CHAPTER 5

The phone conversation with my Maw took place on a Friday evening, which is always the start of my monthly spring break in my crow's nest. After I hung up, I went into the kitchen to do two things: grab a beer and look at the calendar. I look at calendars only when my back is to the wall and I am forced by unavoidable circumstances to see where I stand on the long road to the boneyard. Calendars are like wristwatches, except you can't move a calendar ahead ten minutes, or ten days, or ten months, or ten years. By "can't" I mean you "can," but it just wouldn't be the same thing as yanking the stem of a watch. Right at that moment though, I wished I could rip ten days off the calendar and make it be December 26th.

This was December 16th. If I could have figured out how to rip ten days off Time, I would have done it without hesitation. Then it would be D-26 and I would already be on a plane back to Denver. Right away I started thinking of writing a science fiction novel about a man who travels through time by ripping pages off a calendar. This is what happens to people who want to make money writing novels. I don't know if I've mentioned this to you, but I've been writing novels since I was in college.

I graduated from college when I was twenty-nine years old. I got a free ride from Uncle Sam on the GI Bill. By "free" I mean it cost two years of my life. But in return, I received seven years of doing nothing in school, which brought the total up to nine consecutive years of doing nothing. If you think I'm exaggerating I can get notarized affidavits from teachers and sergeants, but why bother? That would require an effort on my part, which would be detrimental to my perfect record of doing absolutely nothing since high school. Okay. I'll admit it. I've done a few things, but not on purpose.

I went back into the living room and sat down in my easy chair and looked at the television for a moment. It stood in one corner of my living room. Then I looked at my steamer trunk. It was filled with all of my unpublished novels. It rested in another corner. I looked back-and-forth at these two large rectangles trying to decide whether to devote the evening to writing a novel or watching TV. The problem with writing a novel is that it takes a couple of months, whereas *Gilligan's Island* takes thirty minutes. I was torn.

I stared at the two boxes, then I slowly crossed my eyes so that the boxes converged. My steamer trunk suddenly had a TV screen pasted on the front of it. This seemed symbolic to me. I wasn't certain what my eyes were getting at, so I uncrossed them and got up for another beer. I was starting to feel edgy due to the prospect of going home for Christmas.

I had attended Kansas Agricultural University (KAU) after I got out of the army. I got free room and board at home, and I dated a girl named Mary Margaret Flaherty. Mary and I had talked a lot about getting married in the way that hippies in those days talked a lot about buying land and starting a commune. I knew a lot of hippie-types in those days, and I couldn't imagine hitchhiking to a welfare office with any of them, much less living on a farm. It would be like living in an army barracks again, except I would have to milk cows. This is one aspect of the Civil War that never gets mentioned in high school history books. Who milked the cows? There must have been one hell of a lot of cows in the Civil War.

This gave me an idea for a novel. A man figures out a way to travel through time by ripping pages off a calendar, and he ends up in the Civil War where he's put to work milking cows for the Union army. That pretty much took care of the first chapter. Only twenty-nine more to go. This has always been one of my problems with writing novels. I'm good at coming up with first chapters, but then the story starts to sag a bit. Plus, I know nothing about the Civil War, but then I know nothing about practically everything. I did serve in the army though, so I thought I might be able to squeeze a second chapter out of the book by putting in a lot of stuff about screaming sergeants. I did not doubt for one moment that sergeants screamed in the Civil War, and even in the Revolutionary War. Sergeants were probably screaming at Waterloo and in King Arthur's court. The ancient Greeks probably had screaming sergeants. There were probably sergeants screaming while the walls of Jericho were falling down. Maybe I could do a coffee-table book about the history of screaming sergeants.

Instead I looked at my calendar again. This was a bad sign and I knew it. I first started looking at calendars in the army. I probably don't need to go into too much detail explaining why I looked at calendars in the army but I used to sit on my bunk and count the total number of days that I would be required to wear a uniform. No matter how I added it up, it always came out to 730. I even tried a few "tricks" taught to me in high school algebra class. For instance: if $X=2$, then $365X=730$. That wasn't much help. So I tried: if $X=365$, then $2X=730$. I was getting nowhere fast. Then I tried putting the X into parentheses: $2(X)$. I won't bore you with the result. But I will say that after graduating from high school I never used algebra for anything except killing time in the army.

The nun who taught us algebra in high school once told us that the invention of the zero (0) was a major leap in the evolution of mathematics. I liked that. After all, "zero" means "nothing," and I have always been fascinated by the concept of "nothing" because no matter where you look, you can't see nothing.

After studying the calendar, I calculated that I would have to fly to Wichita on the 23nd, a Friday, and stay over until the 26th, a Monday, since Christmas fell on a Sunday. Then I tried to do what I call a little "shaving." Maybe I could arrive in Wichita on the 23rd, and fly out late on the 25th. That would bring my actual stay in Wichita down to forty-eight hours. However, if I arrived at six in the evening on Friday and left at noon on Sunday, I might be able to "shave" my stay down to thirty-six hours. I suddenly felt like I was at the dog track making last-second calculations before the betting window closed.

But it was a fool's ploy and I knew it. Christmas isn't like the Fourth of July or Halloween. It's The Big Kahuna of holidays. When you go home for Christmas, you're in it for the long haul.

I gave it up and went into the bathroom to look at my face in the mirror. I always do that after giving up. I didn't like what I saw. My ponytail was getting a little ragged. I would have to make a trip to Gino's Barbershop before flying home. I hadn't been to Gino's in more than a month, even though one of the barbers, Tony, always gave me free haircuts due to the fact that I had played a key role in helping him recover from a gambling problem awhile back. I tried not to do that on purpose, but my back was to the wall. It was either help him or feel guilty, and I always jump at the opportunity to avoid guilt.

I picked up a hairbrush that Tony's Uncle Gino had once given to me.

"Use only this on your hair," he had insisted.

It was kind of unnerving the way he said it. He was frowning.

He had emigrated from Italy when he was a little boy, so I took him seriously. Who knows, maybe the brush possessed supernatural powers? We're talking old Europe here. I wasn't about to invoke any curses. I get enough of that from my customers.

I brushed my ponytail for a minute, hoping I could convince myself that I wouldn't need to go to Gino's. But I wasn't buying it. The thing is, I hate getting free haircuts. In fact I hate getting anything free. The price is always too high.

I set the brush down and stared at my face in the mirror for a while longer. Going home, I thought to myself. Yep. I'm going home. I started saying it out loud:

"Going home."

"Going home."

Then I started singing it. I'm talking Woodstock of course: Ten Year's After. But I couldn't remember any of the words except, "Going home to see my baby …" This made me think of Mary Margaret Flaherty. It's funny how thinking things makes you think other things. I don't think I've ever thought anything without thinking about something else. This was particularly true in grade school. It started in first grade. At that time I didn't understand that I would have to sit at a desk for twelve years. After one week into the school "experience" my attitude was, "Well, this has been interesting, but I want to go home now and watch TV." That was at Blessed Virgin Catholic Grade School in Wichita. That's where I first met Mary Margaret Flaherty.

I started wondering what had become of Mary Margaret. She moved away from Wichita a couple years after I dropped out of college and moved to Atlanta. I have tried to put her out of my mind, but so far I haven't succeeded in spite of numerous trips to Sweeny's Tavern. But back then I had this idea that I would come back to

Wichita some day as a rich writer and she would be waiting for me. When I went home for my father's funeral she wasn't there, and none of her family showed up to pay their respects.

The Flaherty's lived on the other side of town. My Maw often referred to Mary Margaret as "that little gold-digger." The Flaherty's were considered "lace-curtain Irish." The Murphy's were considered "shanty Irish." I had no idea what made my Maw think Mary Margaret was a gold-digger, since I was perpetually broke. But I figured that if I became a rich writer I would move vertically into the "lace-curtain" category. In theory, this would lift my family out of the gutter and put us on an even keel with the Flaherty's. But so far we're still in the gutter. My sisters married well-to-do businessmen, and my older brother is making money hand-over-fist in California—and of course I'm a professional taxi driver—but for some reason we're still in the gutter. I never have figured that out.

CHAPTER 6

I woke up on Saturday morning, December 17, and peeked through the curtain to gaze upon the dead of winter. The temperature was 79. The sunshine blinded me. Colorado is the most ridiculous state on the weather map. The ski resorts were going broke. On the upside, the people who manufacture snow-making machines were rolling in dough. As I ate my morning hamburger, I watched a TV newscast about people skiing in swimsuits down slopes that were barely frosted with artificial snow that was being fired onto the ground by the machines. By "artificial" I mean "man-made." "Artificial" also means "not real," but you never hear computer nerds admit that "artificial intelligence" means "not-real intelligence." It's always "*man-made* intelligence." They like to pretend that their computers can actually think and that the thinking is "man-made" which, ergo, makes the nerds demigods. Sorry, pals, but "artificial fruit" isn't something you can eat.

As you can see, I was in a bad mood because I was going to ruin spring break by "doing" something. In this case it was getting a haircut. Ironically, I usually drive my taxi on Monday, Wednesday, and Friday, and I have no problem crawling out of bed and going to Rocky Cab on work days. But when Saturday arrives I become bitter and resentful if I have to make the slightest effort to do anything at all. Going to the laundromat is unspeakable. I have to do that once a month. When I was in college I did my laundry in secret so that nobody would know I had imperfections, but let's move on.

I own a lot of T-shirts and blue jeans, as well as socks and underwear. I keep my dirty laundry in a giant box, which is normally referred to as a "closet." Once a month I haul a load down to Blanchards, which is a franchise laundromat that has hundreds of washing machines and dryers. It's on east Colfax. They have a small bar at Blanchards. You can drink beer while-u-wait. Yuppies do their laundry there. It's the hip place to display your imperfections. I always feel ashamed walking into Blanchards carrying thirty pair of dirty underwear. Is that my Catholicism showing, or am I just normal?

I usually do my laundry on the same day I pay my rent. That way I get two things out of the way at the same time. Paying rent takes almost as much effort as doing laundry because I have to go downstairs and knock on my landlord's door. My landlord is actually a kid in his twenties, the manager for the absentee landlord. I give the kid my dough, then I drive to Blanchards. It's a real grind.

At any rate, I had to drive to Gino's Barbershop that day to get my ponytail trimmed. I wanted to get it out of the way before noon. That way I would have the rest of Saturday and all day Sunday to do nothing. The irony is that getting my haircut out of the way was exactly what my Maw used to tell me in reference to doing my homework on Friday night when I was a kid.

"Then ye'll have the whole weekend free to play," she used to say.

I never bought into that when I was a kid, and yet here I was, forty-five years old and trying to get a chore out of the way so I would have the whole weekend free. Was I growing up at last? No. It's because Gino's Barbershop wasn't open at nine o'clock on Sunday night.

But I knew what was really bugging me. The only reason I was getting a haircut was so I would look like a "daycent human baying" as me ol' Mither called well-groomed young men back in my youth. Getting my ponytail trimmed would be the first step in going home. The haircut had suddenly become a "symbol," and as an aspiring writer of commercial fiction I have an aversion to symbolism, which I can't think up anyway.

I put off going to Gino's until it was almost noon, then I finally surrendered. Denial wasn't working so I opted for self-delusion. I pretended it was the last day of the month and I was just "taking care of business." I went to my closet and opened it and looked at my fifteen sets of dirty cabbie clothes. I had decided to pretend that I was going to the laundry. Empty-handed, I walked downstairs using the interior stairwell and strolled past my landlord's door. I pretended to knock on it and hand him a rent check. This got me outside. So far, so good. Then I pretended to carry the load of laundry to my car, sort of staggering with my arms outstretched. At this point two teenage girls walked by and giggled at me. I stood up straight and hurried to my Chevy. Forget psychiatry. If you want to cure yourself of anything, have two teenage girls giggle at you.

I drove down to Colfax and turned east, flipping the visor down so the December sunlight wouldn't burn my retinas. When I came to the stoplight at Colorado Boulevard, I pulled my sunglasses out of my glove compartment. Then I turned on the air conditioner full-blast. I hate winter in Colorado.

Gino's Barbershop is in Aurora, the enchanted suburb. I arrived at twelve-thirty. I drove past the front door and glanced through the window and saw Gino Bombalini working a chair. Gino is the uncle of Tony Bombalini, the man with the former gambling problem. I swung around the block and parked my heap.

"Murph!" Gino hollered when I walked in. "You got a date tonight?"

Gino was convinced that every time I came in for a haircut I was on the road to marriage.

"Not tonight," I said genially. I couldn't help it. Gino made me genial. He had an Italian accent. He reminded me of me ol' Dad, except pop had an Irish accent.

"Have a seat, Murph," Gino said. "I'll be with you in a minute. You look at the girly magazines, eh?"

Gino was convinced that if I looked at the girly magazines lying on his table I would decide to get married. By "girly" magazines I mean *Pro Wrestling*. Once in awhile I might see a snapshot of a babe in a bikini holding up a sign that read "Round 7" in a sports arena where two monstrosities were choking each other on the canvas. This was as X-rated as the girly magazines got at Gino's. He was from the old country.

Gino finished up his current head, a man who looked to me like he didn't really need a haircut and maybe had come in for the conversation. I mention this because professional novelists like to pretend that they notice little things that other people never notice. I pretend that, too. I pay special attention to the obscure parts of the human body that Norman Mailer and James Joyce never expounded upon. I hope to carve a niche for myself in the literary world, and split-ends just might be the key to success.

"All right, Murph, you're next," Gino said, flapping a fresh towel like a bullfighter.

I climbed onto the chair and braced myself for my monthly clip.

"Hey … what's this?" Gino said, peering closely at my ponytail. I froze.

"I have no idea what you are talking about," I said. It sort of leapt from my throat. I had learned the phrase in grade school. It was Pavlovian. I often said it when nuns weren't even yelling at me.

"Why you no use the brush?" Gino said.

"I use the brush," I said.

Gino did a quick snippy thing with the scissors and held up a tiny piece of my ponytail. "Have you been using a comb?"

I started to sweat. Was this the end of my free ride?

"What did I tell you about using the brush?" Gino said.

"I had to do it, Gino," I confessed. "I had to use a comb."

"But why?" he said. "Why you no use the brush like I say?" By now he had come around and was standing in front of me. Gino was shorter than me, but he had big forearms. He was like that guy in *The Godfather.* You know who I mean. The guy with the mustache.

I swallowed hard. "I was waiting outside the Brown Palace Hotel in my taxi two days ago when a beautiful woman came toward my cab. I do not wish to offend you, Gino, but we are both men of the world, and so I will say this to you. She had broad, shapely hips."

Gino dropped his hands to his sides and his eyes got big.

"Her hair was as black as that of a raven," I said. "I had to do it. I pulled out my comb and quickly stroked my ponytail. I did not want her to think I was a bum."

A wan smile spread across Gino's face.

I continued: "And I did not want her to think badly of my barber."

A look of fear came into his eyes.

"I had only enough time to tuck my comb into my briefcase before she climbed in and leaned forward and spoke into my ear. Her breath smelled like Ragu. She said she wanted me to take her to Saint Thomas Aquinas Catholic High School where she was going to help cook a spaghetti dinner for the young men of the C.Y.O."

I lowered my eyes, then glanced up at Gino. He was putty in my hands. "I am fairly certain that she was of Italian extraction."

Gino started to sweat. He got busy working on my ponytail. "Did you get her name?" he said.

"I am sorry to say this, but I did not."

"Why? Why did you not get her name?"

"I was afraid she would know what I was thinking."

Gino stopped clipping. "Hey … wait a minute. Just what were you thinking?" he said judgmentally.

"I was thinking that she would never marry a humble cab driver," I said.

Gino started clipping again, and as he spoke, he smiled. "I think maybe you are playing a joke on me, Murph. You are a cab driver, but you are not humble."

"You caught me, Gino."

"Aaah Murph, don't ever try to fool Gino."

"I promise I will never lie to you again."

"If you want to find a wife, you keep a hairbrush with you at all times," he said.

"I'll make a note of that," I lied. "Where's Tony today?"

"He and Angelina flew to Chicago this morning. They are going to spend Christmas with the family."

"Do you mean The Family or the family?" I said.

"I mean the family," he said.

"Sorry I missed him," I said. "The reason I came in today is because I wanted to look my best when I get back to Wichita. My Maw called and asked me to come home for Christmas."

"You are a good son," Gino said.

"Could you put that in writing?"

"What are you going to give to your mother for Christmas?"

"Huh?"

"What sort of present have you picked out to give to your mother on Christmas morning?"

I had to think fast. He was holding a pair of scissors.

"A ThighMaster," I said.

"What is that?"

"It's a kind of exercise machine for your legs."

"ThighMaster," Gino mused aloud as he finished up. "Thigh-Master. That does not sound like a good thing for a son to give to his mother."

"Well, maybe you're right. Maybe I'll give her a fruitcake."

He nodded. But he had opened a door that heretofore had been closed. It hadn't occurred to me that I might be expected to hand out presents at Christmas. The word "onerous" welled up in my mind. I couldn't remember the last time I had given anybody a present. My only actual memory of giving out presents took place when I was ten years old. It involved an afternoon of playing Skee-Ball. Remind me to tell you my Skee-Ball story sometime.

After I got out of the chair, Gino and I enacted a small vignette that we always go through at the end of a clip: first I pull out my billfold and try to pay him, but he waves me off. Then I try to tip him, and he pretends to get angry. Then I surrender and put my billfold away.

I hate that vignette. Gino was a close friend though, so I always played the scene out to the end. Whenever I offer money to friends or acquaintances or strangers and they wave it off, my money immediately goes back into my billfold. This usually shocks them, and also explains why I have so few friends. Conversely, if a friend offers me money, I instantly take it. This is even more shocking. But to me, the idea that I could be more generous than somebody else is so ludicrous that I just want to get the farce over with.

"You have a merry Christmas!" Gino said as I walked toward the door. "And do not give your mother a ThighBlaster!"

"Merry Christmas, Gino," I replied. I pulled the door open and stepped onto the sun-baked streets of Aurora. I put on my shades and hurried to the car before the Yuletide heat brought me to my knees.

CHAPTER 7

Here's the punchline:
It snowed on December 23rd.

I'm talking record-depth. So rather than drive my heap to DIA and leave it in long-term parking, which I had planned to do, I called Yellow Cab. I didn't want to put a Rocky Cab driver through the onerous job of plowing his way twenty-five miles to the airport, even though it would have been a good score for a brother cabbie. But also, I didn't trust a Rocky driver to show up at my door on time. Let's just leave that one alone.

The Yellow driver kept glancing at my face in his rearview mirror as we made our way up Colorado Boulevard toward Interstate 70. Then he asked me if I had ever been to Los Angeles. I said no. He looked surly. I think he recognized me. The thing is, I once cost the entire Denver cab-driving fleet an enormous amount of money when they bet against me on what they thought was a sure-thing, and they lost. It's a long story. I don't want to talk about it.

I don't want to talk about the wait at DIA either. The planes were stacked up. When DIA was being built, the citizens of Denver were promised that the old days of waiting out snowstorms were over. We sat in the 727 for three hours waiting for the snowplows to clear the futuristic Buck Rogers whiz-bang laser-beam runways of DIA. By the time we were in the air, I had broken my vow to stay sober until I got to Wichita. As a consequence I was well into the Christmas spirit by the time we landed.

The reason I originally had wanted to remain sober until I arrived in Wichita was so I could rent a car. I had no intention of being
trapped in the Murphy house without a means of escape. I intended
to rent a hotel room a few miles from home. You don't spend twenty
years avoiding friends, relatives, and sergeants without picking up
a few "tricks" along the way. But I decided to hold off renting a car
until the next day. I could still smell the flight-scotch drifting off my
lips and I knew that the car-rental clerk would laugh me out of the
office if I breathed on him right then and I hate being laughed at. It
gets old.

I hauled my one suitcase out to the sidewalk and waited for a
Yellow Cab to pull up first in line. Whenever I leave Denver and
travel to another city I always take Yellow Cabs. In the world of big
business, this approach to consumerism is referred to as "name recognition." When I wrote brochures for Dyna-Plex I used the phrase
"name recognition" all the time, even though I had no idea what sort
of product or services Dyna-Plex provided for its customers, whoever
they were. But I got a lot of mileage out of "name recognition" and
the bosses, whoever they were, never complained, which in my world
was equivalent to effusive praise.

A Yellow Cab pulled up to the terminal and the driver hopped
out and opened his trunk. I hoisted the suitcase in and he slammed
the trunk shut and ran back to the driver's seat. I climbed into the
backseat.

"Where to?" he said.

"Downtown Holiday," I replied.

He nodded and started his meter, then pulled away from the
terminal.

"Where did you fly in from?" he said.

A standard cabbie question. It was like a crowbar that all asphalt warriors use to pry open a fare's mouth and get him talking so the driver can turn off his mind and spend the rest of the trip nodding and saying things like, "I hear you, man," without actually hearing anything.

"I came in from Denver," I replied.

"What do you do there?" he said.

"I drive a taxi," I said.

The Yellow driver glanced at my face in the rearview mirror. He took hold of the mirror and wiggled it up and down to get a better look at me.

"Is your name Murph?" he said.

"No."

He frowned at me, then looked back at the road.

Fer the luvva Christ—Big Al must have been taking bets on the short-wave. He was the guy who had made book on me during the L.A. debacle.

We rode the rest of the way in silence. I kept my hand on the door handle just in case.

When we arrived at the Holiday I quickly climbed out. The driver opened the trunk and hauled out my suitcase. I kept my face averted as I handed him the money and mumbled, "Keep the change."

I walked into the hotel keeping my head bowed. I was already thinking I might have to move to another hotel. The Word would be out by dawn.

I told the clerk I would be staying until the 26th and that I would be in and out for the next couple of days. I paid him in advance. I could tell he liked that. Desk clerks and cabbies have a lot in common, like "grave doubt." After I got settled in my room, I went back to the lobby and looked outside. I hid behind a tripod holding a poster announcing a band that would be appearing in the hotel lounge over the holidays. They called themselves The Bio Rhythms.

The Yellow driver was gone. There was a Checker Cab parked at the cabstand now, so I went to my room and grabbed my suitcase and left the hotel, giving the clerk a brief wave as I walked by. He probably pegged me as an anvil salesman, or a drug lord.

"Where to?" the Checker driver said.

I gave him an intersection in my old neighborhood. I wanted him to drop me off nowhere near the family home.

He dropped me off at an intersection along Douglas Avenue, a half-mile from home. When I was ten, this intersection was my "stomping" grounds, although it's kind of hard to "stomp" when you weigh fifty pounds. I was the skinniest kid at Blessed Virgin Catholic Grade School but I never had any trouble with bullies. No bully with an ounce of pride wanted to be known as "the hood that pounded Brendan Murphy." Even the eggheads ostracized me. The truth is, I didn't have any friends in grade school. I was too naive at the time to realize what a sweet deal that was. I drifted through my childhood virtually invisible. The invisibility made it a lonely trek, but also made it easy to peek at girly magazines.

After I paid the cabbie, I set my suitcase on the sidewalk and stood for a moment at the intersection. I realized I had done much the same thing after I dropped out of KAU and headed for Atlanta. I had hopped into my car and drove as far as this intersection, where I got a flat tire. But back then I had no college degree and no future. Now I have a college degree.

A lot of shops and stores were clustered at the intersection. It was like a miniature town, a neighborhood shopping district European in flavor. Everything you needed to survive was right there within walking distance of home: a couple drugstores, a Safeway, a movie theater, a medical clinic, a toy store, a gas station, all the cozy little places of business where everybody knew everybody else. But most of the businesses had since been destroyed by the same malls that have made strangers out of almost everybody in America, thank goodness.

I picked up my suitcase and began walking up Douglas. I passed the Roxy Theater. I had spent most of my Saturdays at the Roxy. They had a free show on Saturday from nine until noon, and then regular feature films in the afternoon. The Roxy was the place where I attended my first movie at night, six to eight p.m. I was ten years old. It made me feel like a grownup to attend a movie at night. I saw the 1960 British film, *Jack the Ripper.* It scared the hell out of me. I had to walk home in the dark. I never wanted to feel like a grownup again.

I came to the intersection of my street and headed south, even though it felt like "west" but don't ask me to explain why. When I was in the Boy Scouts, reading a compass was like holding an algebra in my hand. Don't ask me to explain that either.

Home was three blocks away, and as I passed the houses on the final leg of the journey, I looked at each structure and was reminded of some incident related to it. Here's the house where the German Shepherd snapped at me. Here's the house where the old lady gave me rock candy on Halloween. I gave it to the German Shepherd. Here's the house where the teenage girls giggled at me. As far as I know, they didn't cure me of anything.

I crossed the street to the block where the Murphy house was located. As I walked along, the other houses damn near started whispering, "He's back." This block was my entire world up until the age of four, when I finally learned how to cross a street. A neighborhood ruffian showed me how to do it. When we got to the other side I was wracked with guilt. Have I ever mentioned that I'm Irish-Catholic?

After I ran back to my side of the street, I was certain that my Maw had seen me *breaking a rule!!!* Even if she hadn't seen me, I knew God would drop by later to tell her.

Luckily I got away with it.

Or did I?

For some reason, me ol' Dad never entered into these rule-breaking scenarios. Throughout my childhood he was just a tall, silent person who sort of came and went. I never quite understood what his purpose around the house was, until I turned seven years old and he announced that I was of a proper age to receive a weekly allowance. That's when I realized me ol' Dad's purpose in life was to give me a quarter.

CHAPTER 8

It was nearing eight o'clock at night, the neighborhood was dark and cold, and low clouds were moving in. It looked like Wichita was going to have a white Christmas again this year. I couldn't remember a childhood Christmas when it *didn't* snow. In Denver you have a fifty-fifty chance of a snowstorm or a heat wave. Did I ever mention that Denver has dry snow and Wichita has wet snow? Don't ask me what dry snow is, I'm no rocket scientist. These were the thoughts I was having as I stood before the old family home, killing time by trying to get up the nerve to prove Thomas Wolfe was wrong while simultaneously wishing he was right.

Let's get the descriptive prose out of the way. The Murphy house is two stories tall, made of white clapboard, and has a front porch. The house was built in 1900, like the rest of America. There's a driveway made of two parallel concrete strips that run toward a garage at the rear of the house. Grass grows between the strips of concrete. The backyard has never had any grass but it does have a tree. The tree is tall and plays a major role in a story about the time I talked my evil brother Gavin into jumping off the roof of our garage. Remind me to tell you that story sometime. My brother is one year older than me. He became an Eagle Scout at the age of twelve. I remained a Tenderfoot. He lives in California and is no longer involved in scouting. Neither am I, as far as I know.

I climbed the steps and crossed the porch to the door and leaned in close to give a listen. Habit. I always leaned in to listen when I was a kid. I once walked into the house while my mother was having tea with Monsignor O'Leary, who asked me why I hadn't shown up at school the previous Saturday morning to begin studying to become an altar boy. Once burned, twice shy, that's all I have to say about that intrusion.

Well, it looked like I was going to have to go into my "Brendan" act. This differs from my "cab driver" act, which I utilize when chauffeuring strangers around the mean streets of Denver. My Brendan act is the character I play when I'm around my siblings. I have to pretend I'm their brother. The amount of energy this uses up is mind-boggling. Like a football player involved in a brutal championship game, I expected to drop ten pounds before I left Wichita.

I braced myself for the moment when I would have to act surprised upon stepping into the living room and finding everyone seated on chairs grinning at me with unconcealed delight. I cannot bear unconcealed delight.

I shoved the door open and stepped into the house.

And was met with total silence.

This was not an unfamiliar experience. It often happens when I go to parties at my friends' houses, especially when I haven't been invited. But on this particular night there was a different reason for the silence: nobody was there.

Right next to the front door was a small table where my Maw had been leaving notes since the day she got married. I spotted the piece of paper instantly. It was almost as bad as encountering a person, but not as bad as a telephone call.

"Boy-o," the note began. "Cold-cuts in the fridge. Stay out of the liquor cabinet. We are at the school play. Your niece Becky is a wise man."

No need for Maw to elaborate. I knew the school play routine.

I had once been in a Christmas pageant at Blessed Virgin Grade School. I played a pine tree, but let's move on.

I knew that having read the note I would be expected to show up to catch the end of the school play, assuming I read it before the family got home. I put the note back on the table exactly as I had found it. This was a "trick" I used to pull when I was a kid to make my Maw think I hadn't seen any of the notes she left lying around, in case she ordered me to do something that I ended up not doing, like cleaning my room or getting a job.

I picked up my suitcase and walked through the silent house feeling as if I was walking through a museum. The old place looked exactly as it had when I was growing up, as it had when I got out of the army and moved back in so I could go to school rent-free on the GI Bill. I knew the layout so well that I could have walked through the house in total darkness and not stumbled over anything, which I frequently did after I began "borrowing" booze from the liquor cabinet during my college days.

I did stop at the liquor cabinet, a fancy piece of furniture made of mahogany. I opened the little wooden doors. All of the liquor bottles had horizontal lines sketched along the edges. Maw was still using the same ol' Magic Marker.

It was good to be back home.

The Christmas tree had been set up by the staircase. Glass balls. Tinsel. Lights. You've seen Christmas trees.

I climbed the stairs to my bedroom, where I stowed my suitcase. I sat down on the bed for a moment and looked around at the walls where my Beach Boy posters were still hanging. The Sixties would never die on my watch. I got up and went back downstairs. I found cold-cuts in the fridge and made a sandwich out of Wonder Bread. When I was a child, Wonder Bread built strong bodies eight ways.

But then, when I got older, it began building strong bodies twelve ways. I was intrigued by this startling advance in science, and I have to admit that my fascination with Madison Avenue has never fully left me.

After I finished the sandwich, I searched the fridge for something else to eat—not that I was hungry, I was just stalling in order to avoid walking to the old school to meet the family. A kind of lethargy had set in, the same sort of lethargy that often affected me in Denver when it was snowing and I knew I was going to be making money hand-over-fist because everybody in town would be calling cabs. It was a sure thing. Sure things always make me lazy. This was why it took me so long to get around to completing a novel manuscript when I was in college. I was sure that as soon as I mailed the manuscript to a publisher I would be receiving a check for fifty grand, which would allow me to drop out of college, move to an island in the Pacific, and continue to peck out novels while lying on a hammock.

Back then I planned to use my first advance to buy a small portable Smith Corona, which would rest lightly on my belly as I typed. I spent a great deal of time practicing writing novels while lying on my bed with my head and my feet resting on thick pillows—my "Hammock Simulator" as it were. The beauty of the hammock is that you are not lying perfectly prone, but rather resting in a kind of half-moon posture, which allows you to balance a typewriter on your midsection while leaving your arms free to reach for the daiquiri on the table next to the hula girl.

I finally gave up pretending to look for something to eat. There was no use putting it off. I had to hike over to my old school and experience the hell in hello.

I left the house and walked back toward Douglas Avenue, and

felt the first cold sprinkles of damp snow tickling my face. Something told me I would be the person using the snow shovel in the morning. That ineffable "something" was the voice of my Maw. Snow shoveling was one of my chores when I lived rent-free at home. My other chore was mowing the lawn in the summer. I dreaded those seasons. I tried to talk my Maw into buying a large dog so the lawn would be killed by his fertilization techniques, but my Maw was onto my plan from the start and wouldn't spring for a new hound. Our old dog, a sheltie named Shelteen, had simply been too little to kill the lawn—although God knows I fed her enough Alpo to kill a golf course.

I took the side streets toward Blessed Virgin, the same route I had walked for twelve years to grade school and high school. The high school is across the street from the grade school. During the eighth grade the nuns started us in on this deal that they called the "interdepartmental system," which involved moving from classroom to classroom every hour for different subjects. This was to help us make the psychological transition from grade school to high school. Apparently the nuns believed that if we didn't get used to picking up our books at the end of each hour and walking to a different classroom we would succumb to shock when we entered high school, where the interdepartmental system had been established in the 1940s to prepare the students mentally for the trauma of college. That may sound a bit melodramatic, but the interdepartmental system did prepare me for the trauma of moving from job to job.

The houses started whispering again as I walked to school. Here's the house where the hobo was asleep under the porch. Here's the house where the kid with three ears lived. Here's the alley where I smoked my first cig. I felt like Beaver Cleaver come home—except there was no Larry Mondello in my life. I did recall at least three Eddie Haskells in my life, and one Lumpy Rutherford, but no Larry

Mondello. Okay. I'll admit it. *I* was Larry Mondello. I talked other kids into doing things that they got into trouble for, while I ran away. Did I mention the fact that I talked my brother into jumping off our garage roof? As soon as I sized up the breadth of that calamity I ran to the Roxy Theater on the off-chance that there would be a big blowup at home. In the event of blowups I always denied everything. And just as in the brilliant sitcoms of Joe Connelly and Bob Mosher, it never worked. My Maw was a lot like Larry Mondello's mother in those days. "Just wait until your father gets home," she was fond of saying. My Maw liked to watch *Leave it to Beaver* with me, so she was up-to-speed on my antics. I don't think anything made my Maw quite as happy as becoming enraged at the sight of June Cleaver vacuuming the living room wearing pearls.

"Yeh notice that the little Beaver boy-o never gets spanked," she used to say at the end of each episode. This made us both laugh, although mine was hollow laughter.

CHAPTER 9

As I drew closer to Blessed Virgin Parish, I began to feel myself regressing to the age of ten. I bypassed the age of twenty-two because when I was living at home and going to college, my Maw pretty much left me on my own, although "ignored" says it best.

I've often wondered if dropping out of college and going out on my own and traveling around the country and working low-paying jobs and being broke most of the time was a mistake—or mistakes. I've always had trouble with the plural. Why is the word "group" singular when it means a bunch of people? Anyway, the idea was—and still is—that I would become a rich novelist someday, so I'm kind of withholding judgment on the mistake(s) deal. I'm not sure what the deadline is on becoming an official failure, but I assume it's either sixty-five or death, rough estimate.

Then it came in sight, the ol' parish. The place was lit up due to the Christmas pageant. All right, here's my Christmas pageant story:

Blessed Virgin grade school was putting on a Christmas play that involved a man chopping down pine trees. That's as much of the plot as I can remember. Me and three other kids were cast as the pine trees. My evil brother Gavin had the job of narrating the play in iambic pentameter. He stood at the edge of the stage under a spotlight wearing a new suit that my mother had bought him for the occasion. I was dressed in jeans and a flannel shirt and had pine branches sewn to my clothes. I was a Blue Spruce. When the kid/man with the cardboard axe came around and pretended to chop at my stump, my job was to fall over. It was the easiest gig I ever pulled. One chop and I was lumber.

After the play, we trees were sent into the first grade classroom to change out of our clothes, but I was too embarrassed to change in front of the other kids so I kept my pine needles on for the rest of the evening—I was six years old and I was a Catholic. The needles itched like hell. Gavin didn't change either, but he was wearing a suit. He looked like David Niven compared to me, but who doesn't? He floated around the gymnasium after the show being charming to the nuns while I stood in the shadows and scratched. I've hated someone ever since and I assume it's Gavin. Why couldn't the nuns have picked *me* to narrate the play!

Ah, what the hell, that was thirty-nine years ago. Why dwell on the pageant? Gavin has given me better reasons to hate him since then. For instance, his draft number was so high that he was never called up for the service. I was something like #1 in the lottery. As a result, while I was wearing the uniform of our country and nursing beers in Tennessee strip joints, Gavin was nursing beers in Kansas strip joints. The injustice was infuriating.

I made my way around to the entrance of the gymnasium where the play was being held. A lot of men were standing around outside having smokes—bored fathers of the kids inside. When I was a kid there had been a lot more cigarettes, and half the smokes were cigars. But times have changed. I imagine that twenty years from now the fathers will be jogging in place. The health nuts of this country have taken the romance out of boredom.

"He's here!" someone barked.

The men grabbed me and hauled me toward the lighted doorway.

"You got the wrong guy!" I shouted out of habit.

They escorted me into the foyer of the gymnasium, which was

crowded with fathers who didn't smoke. The interior doors of the gym were open and I could see the pageant taking place on the stage. The auditorium was dark but the stage was a rectangle of purple light. I'll say one thing for the Christmas pageants, when it came to form they always looked good. The "theater nuns" were masters at staging shows. They understood lighting techniques, creating appropriate atmosphere, and generally fashioning a visually pleasing performance. The content, on the other hand, never came off as well, but then hasn't this always been true of art? I can't tell you how many times in college I sat through a beautiful yet boring production of *Hamlet*. Yes I can. Three. But let's move on.

"He's here!" somebody yelled again. A chill ran down my spine, as it always does when anybody knows I'm anywhere. I'm sure there must be a psychological reason for this, since I can't imagine any other reason.

We passed into the rear of the auditorium and the voices became whispers, "He's here, he's here." There must have been thirty people surrounding me. It reminded me of the moment Ruby shot Oswald. I'll give you one guess who Oswald was. Ruby turned out to be Maw—she came at me out of nowhere.

"Boy-o, yeh made it!" she said. "I knew I could count on yeh."

If you want to know what my Maw looks like, think of Ma Joad, or Ma Kettle, then add Opie's mother in *The Music Man*. What the hell, you might as well throw Ma Barker into the mix—and if you happen to know anything about Dylan Thomas' wife, Caitlin, you can sprinkle some of her on top.

She was grinning as she came toward me with her arms outstretched, which really put me off because we Murphys had never been what you would call a "hugging" family. We were more of a "handshaking" family. Any time the Murphys get together for a wedding or a funeral, you're in for one hell of a lot of handshaking.

Instead of hugging me though, Maw grabbed my arm and said, "Yer on in five minutes," and dragged me back out of the auditorium and down a hallway.

"What's going on, Maw?" I said.

She glanced at me. "Mister Olsen is drunk."

Everything snapped into focus.

Mister Olsen was the school janitor. He was the man the nuns called upon whenever a student threw up during class. He had been mopping vomit off the floorboards since I was six. Grade school vomiting is one of the precious memories of childhood that most people tend to forget as they grow older. Outside of saloons, you rarely see adults vomit. My childhood consisted of scrapes, bruises, nuns, homework, bicycles, and vomit.

"Oh no ya don't!" I snarled, wrenching my arm free.

"He can't go on tonight!" Maw said. "Yeh got to do it for the sake of the children!"

I don't know if you're following this, but Maw and I had been on the same wavelength since my conception, so there was no need for her to explain. Mister Olsen had gotten drunk and therefore I was being "asked" to hand out Christmas presents to the kids up on the stage at the end of the pageant dressed as Santa Claus.

"Yeh got the experience," Maw growled, snatching at my wrists. "Yeh told me so yerself."

That's what I got for squawking about the Dyna-Plex disaster. Telling a member of my family about any personal experience was always a risk.

Let me clarify:

When I was a kid I never let any of my siblings know if I had money or candy. I especially didn't let Maw know because she was one of those matriarchs who was fond of saying, "Share with your sisters."

Share.

What a word.

Only a mother would invent a word like "share."

Four minutes later I was dressed in a Santa Claus costume that I figured had been sewn together in 1956 and hadn't been washed since. It held a faint odor of that sweet-smelling sawdust that janitors sprinkle on vomit.

It made me wonder who Mister Olsen really was. Maybe he had gotten the job as janitor when he was a young man, maybe during the Great Depression when there were no other jobs available and he stayed on at BVP all those years because he was grateful for the honest labor. Or maybe he was a violent criminal on parole and the judge ordered him to remain in the custody of the nuns for the remainder of his life on earth, like most Catholics.

After I put on my Santa costume, I looked at myself in a small mirror hanging on the door. I adjusted my beard, straightened my hat, and asked myself why I was living.

The pageant had come to an end. I could hear people milling around in the auditorium waiting for the big Santa moment to start. Santa handed out gifts only to the first graders in this deal. I suppose it made the second graders feel grownup not to get presents, i.e., "that's for the little kids." The nuns were always crabbing at us students to "act mature," and deprivation of joy seemed to be one of the key instructional methods on our road to young Catholic adulthood. I've often wondered how Protestants deal with maturity.

Just before I got to the entrance of the auditorium, I saw a little kid standing behind the door, which was propped open. He was sort of in the shadows. He looked like a tree and he was scratching. The image of him cowering behind the door didn't register until I walked past him, so I started to go back to take another look—then I stopped myself. All of a sudden I didn't want to see him. Or to put it another way, I did want to see him. But I was afraid that if I looked again he wouldn't be there. Instead I took refuge in an old cabbie proverb: When things start turning cosmic, keep driving.

I stepped into the gymnasium.

CHAPTER 10

I walked up onto the stage and sat on a chair in the center where a studio spotlight was aimed at me. Green bags containing small presents surrounded the chair. My job was to reach in and grab a package at random and hand it to a kid as he or she marched past.

At first it was fun. It made me feel like a rich man handing out gifts, a king bloated with largesse. But as the silent kids came at me with their eyes wide with fear and their hands trembling with the excitement of getting a gift, a dark cloud began to settle on my shoulders. What kind of a tradition was this anyway? I mean, I knew the Three Wise Men connection and all that, but did the kids actually think I was real? The answer is yes. I remembered my own first-grade encounter with Santa Claus (Mister Olsen). I was baffled by the fact that Santa had shown up in Wichita. Santa was supposed to sneak into your house on Christmas Eve, so what was he doing at BVP one week ahead of schedule? Did Monsignor O'Leary fly him in from the North Pole? It made me damn uneasy. I was only six years old, and that's pretty young to be feeling damn uneasy.

I continued reaching into the various bags like an automaton and handing presents to the little kids. Thank God I was a cab driver—I had my trademark fake smile nailed to my mug. Most of the little girls mumbled a wispy, "Thank you, Santa," but the boys just took the money and ran. I liked that. When it comes to boys, fear always trumps courtesy.

The show came to an end just as I was beginning to enjoy it

again, but that's true of most things in life. A nun put "Joy to the World" on the PA system and everybody in the audience began applauding wildly. I sat there under the spotlight feeling like a guest on the *Dick Cavett Show*—a world-famous author with a best-selling book under his shiny black belt. I stretched it out a bit, smiling and waving to the faces in the audience and saying "Ho ho ho!" until two nuns dragged me offstage. This I was used to.

They led me to the janitor's closet. I was so dazzled by my performance that I didn't really get a good look at the nuns until they were in the process of slamming the door to my dressing room. I recognized one of the nuns. She had been my teacher in the sixth grade. Her name was Sister Mary Francis. She once got really mad at me. I won't keep you in suspense. Here's my Sister Mary Francis story:

It all started when I stood on top of my desk.

This was back in the early days of the astronaut program, meaning Mercury—I'm talking Redstone rockets and the solo pioneers of lethal employment. Every time an astronaut was scheduled to be launched, a television was brought into our classroom so we could see "living history," the bugbear of all teachers. Some kid's mom would bring the TV from home. A television in school nowadays is no big deal, but in the early '60s it was a mind-blower (see: hippies.) Maybe that's what made my brain go right out the window. Everybody got giddy when the TV was plugged in and turned on. Jaysus! A television in the *classroom*. While we waited for the countdown to start, Sister Mary Francis got up and said she would be right back. Whenever she left the classroom she never told us where she was going, but I always figured she was headed for the lavatory. What a word.

After she walked out the door, the students started talking and laughing and generally cutting up. No nun, and a TV flickering at the front of the room. Kids were leaving their desks and wandering around cracking jokes and tossing paper airplanes, etc. I felt like I was going to explode with excitement. The next thing I knew I was climbing on top of my desk. I stood there grinning at everybody—but like I said, I didn't have any friends in grade school so I didn't know if anybody paid any attention to my antic. As I grinned around the room my eyes fell on the door, which had a high window, and I saw Sister Mary Francis looking right at me. All I could see were her eyes. I had forgotten that this was a ploy of hers whenever she left the classroom. She always sneaked back to check up on us.

Wellsir, the door flew open and Sister Mary Francis came charging into the room like a locomotive. It was at this point that I lost control of my bladder. She grabbed my arm and dragged me off the desk, dragged me to the front of the room, and dragged me out the door. As I say, getting dragged around by nuns was nothing new.

I had no idea what she was going to do to me, but the fact that we were in a wide hallway indicated that she wanted plenty of room to maneuver.

My mind was sort of empty at that point, unlike my pants, but instead of corporal punishment she told me to go get my older brother. "I wish to speak with him," she said sternly.

I wandered up the hallway feeling as I imagine Dostoevsky felt on his way to the firing squad. I knocked on the seventh-grade classroom door, and when Gavin came out I told him Sister Mary Francis wanted to talk to him.

"Why?" he said.

As we walked side-by-side down the hallway I told him that Sister Mary Francis had caught me standing on top of my desk.

The look on his face was indescribable, so I won't.

When we got to the nun, she told me to go into the classroom. Gavin remained outside with her.

I went in and sat down with Fyodor and stared at the top of Sister Mary Francis' head bobbing in the hallway. Sister Mary Francis was the tallest nun I had ever encountered. When I stood directly in front of her she resembled the Matterhorn. The shortest nun at BVP used to slap the boys with regularity. She was born in 1890. She referred to us as "little gangsters." I knew only one girl who ever got slapped. Her name was Deborah Weigand. She grew up to be a hippie.

Anyway, Sister Mary Francis came into the classroom and sat down at her desk without looking at me. The astronaut got launched. I don't remember which astronaut. Maybe Gus. When the school day ended I raced outside and stood in front of the big double doors and waited for my brother to come out. When he did, I intercepted him and demanded to know what Sister Mary Francis had said to him in the hallway.

"She told me that you are the most unruly and disruptive boy in the class," Gavin said. "Then she told me to tell Maw that you stood on top of your desk."

Gavin started laughing. I won't dwell on it. It took him a minute to recover. This was the guy, by the way, who jumped off our garage roof.

But I couldn't believe the nun had said that. I had never thought of myself as "disruptive." It's true that when she was teaching arithmetic I would hold whispered conversations at the back of the classroom with a kid named Donald. He was the only kid who ever spoke to me in grade school, although I would not define him as a friend—more of a "cohort." We would discuss the finer points of *Thriller*, hosted by Boris Karloff, while the nun explained long division, which frankly I did not feel was any different from short division. But to me, "disruptive" meant setting off firecrackers, or stuffing frogs down the backs of girl's dresses. This may have been a problem of semantics.

"You're not going to tell on me are you?" I said.

"Nah," he said, and he meant it. Gavin was a rat in many ways, but we had a kind of unwritten code of kid ethics when it came to dealing with grownups. There was a line you never crossed. You never told on your brother, or a friend, when it came to the truly bad stuff. I would imagine that most brothers share to some degree this unarticulated sense of mutual protection—like soldiers in a war: if the compound is overrun, you stand back-to-back and go down firing, taking as many of the bastards with you as—well, I seem to have gotten off the track here.

The code of honor wore off after an hour. Gavin went ahead and told on me. This didn't bother me. An hour was all I expected out of Gavin's sense of loyalty. I braced myself. But Maw didn't hit the ceiling. She started laughing. It wasn't even maniacal laughter, the kind you might expect to come from someone who has been pushed over the edge and has completely lost her mind (see: Jonathan Harker). It was just regular mom laughter. This did not in any way help me to understand grownups.

But I didn't ask questions. I just slipped out to the drugstore and crawled inside a bottle of soda and tried to forget.

To my knowledge, the man who gave me a quarter every week never even heard about this incident. But if he had heard it, he probably would have been either baffled or indifferent, the two best characteristics of fathers.

Anyway, as the door to the janitor's closet slammed in my face, I noted with interest that Sister Mary Francis wasn't as tall as she used to be. She was a hell of a lot older though. She must have been in her eighties by this time. When I was in sixth grade she had seemed pretty old to me, but then that was also true of Patty McCormack, the child star of *The Bad Seed*. I first saw that movie when I was seven years old, which is probably never a good idea.

I removed Mister Olson's costume and hung it up. I leaned toward the door and listened for a long time, fearful that Sister Mary Francis might have recognized me and would be waiting in the hallway to complete some "unfinished business." Maw never did contact her to discuss my unruly behavior. She took nuns even less seriously than I did.

When I opened the door the coast was clear, so I headed back to the gymnasium. Standing in the foyer were a number of my relatives. "Number" is the right number because there were a lot of them, including my sisters, their children and husbands, my Maw, and of course, my evil brother Gavin. He was chewing on a toothpick and gazing at me with his head cocked at an angle. Gavin has one of those Irish faces that seem set in a permanent smirk, although it's merely bone structure. If his smirk didn't exist though, he would have ordered one by Fed Ex.

"Ya look like ya could use a drink, kid," he said.

I nodded. Gavin and I hadn't seen each other in years, but I knew my brother well, and he wasn't talking bottled soda.

CHAPTER 11

O kay. Here's the garage story.

Gavin was eleven years old and I was ten. He was on the cusp of becoming an Eagle Scout and I was in Year Three of being a Tenderfoot. Little did I realize that I would never make it to Second-Class Scout before I mustered out of the service. That's because I wasn't prescient when I was a kid. Things are different now.

Gavin and I were messing around in the backyard, swinging back and forth on a twenty-foot length of rope tied to a branch of a tall tree that stood in the middle of the yard. There was no grass in the yard, it was just dirt. Gavin possessed a merit badge in knot tying, so he had climbed up the tree and tied the rope to the branch. It was a good knot. The knot plays no further role in this story.

Gavin and I had just come home from the morning show at the Roxy Theater. The feature had been *Tarzan and the She-Devil* starring Lex Barker. Leonard Maltin gives it one and a half stars. He describes it as "boring hokum." You can take that to the bank. But when I was ten years old, I didn't know the difference between Ingmar Bergman and Hal Roach. Things haven't changed much.

So there we were, Gavin and Cheetah taking turns swinging back and forth on the rope, pretending we weren't in Wichita. That's one fantasy I've never outgrown. I would run at the rope, grab it, and try to swing as high as I could in imitation of Tarzan traveling through the jungle on a vine. But the weight and mass of a ten-year-old boy did not translate into effective escapism, so Gavin went into the house and brought out a kitchen chair. Maw didn't see him do this. There were a lot of things Maw never saw when we were kids, but keep that under your hat.

Each of us would take turns standing on the chair, leaping off it, and getting a good ride. We did this until we were bored out of our skulls. It was at this point that I got my bright idea.

"Why don't we swing down off the garage roof?" I said.

By "we" I meant "Gavin." He glanced at the roof, sizing up the situation. I knew he was doing this because he had the same look in his eyes that he always got when he began engineering the acquisition of another merit badge.

"Gee, I don't know," he said, "that's pretty high."

I couldn't believe it.

Doubt.

When I was ten years old I equated doubt with cowardice. I wrote the book.

"Come on, Gavin, you can do it," I said.

"Why don't *you* do it?" he said.

Little did he realize that he was playing right into my hands. "Because I'm scared," I said. On the surface this may have sounded like a shameful admission, but as any ten year old knows, it takes an awfully brave kid to admit he's chicken. By confessing weakness, I had triggered something in Gavin. He saw an opportunity to show me up. The psychology textbooks refer to this ploy as "passive-aggression" but I call it "goading Gavin."

The next thing he knew he was sitting on the edge of the garage roof clutching the end of the rope. The distance from the roof to the ground was twelve feet. The rope was twenty feet long. You do the math.

Gavin sat staring at the ground for five minutes while I roamed around the yard like a troll encouraging him to make the swing. "Come on, what are you waiting for?" I barked. I was pretending to be one of the kids at recess who were always yelling at me to get my head out of my rump. That's how Catholic kids cuss.

Gavin was sort of an arithmetic genius, so I don't know what went wrong with his calculations, but suddenly he did it. He clutched the rope tightly and shoved off from the roof. His knees ricocheted off the ground. But because he was still clutching the rope, and because the laws of physics are indifferent to the sad plight of humanity, the momentum of his drop translated into a "swing" that dragged him across the yard. Did I mention that Gavin was wearing cutoff jeans? His bare knees plowed fresh furrows into the pioneer earth of old Kansas. Up he swung, and back down again for another pass.

I was speechless.

Yet still he clung to the rope. By now an eerie warble was coming from his throat like a longhorn being branded—a moo of despair.

His jaw was jacked wide open and his eyes were like ping-pong balls.

His back-and-forth journey finally came to an end, the rope hanging perpendicular to the branch, yet still he clung—kneeling, bleeding, mooing. Then I heard the screen door slam open.

Maw was coming.

I don't remember running. I only remember entering the dark auditorium of the Roxy Theater and sitting through a feature film that I will never remember barring therapeutic hypnosis.

That was the first time in my life that I realized someday I would have to leave home.

Let's get this over with.

When I came back to the house after dark, my parents were seated in the living room watching Lawrence Welk. I entered through the back door. This is what a ten-year-old boy thinks of as a "strategic maneuver." I slipped upstairs and found Gavin lying on his bed reading a comic book. Both of his knees were wrapped in bandages. I glanced quickly around the room for the telltale sign of crutches. I was afraid my brother had become a paraplegic, although that word was not yet in my vocabulary, but my brain knew what I was getting at.

"Is Maw mad at me?" I said. Me ol' Dad did not enter into this conversation. Fathers are like the Golem of Jewish legend: they come alive only after a kid gets his driver's license.

"She told me to tell you to come downstairs as soon as you snuck home," Gavin said with a smirk.

There was only one thing to do.

"I thought you were *dead!*" I wailed, and I collapsed in a pool of tears. It worked. Maw heard the theatrical crash that I intentionally made as I hit the wooden floor. She rushed upstairs to investigate. When she saw my tear-streaked face she caved in. Moms are pushovers.

The Tarzan Debacle was the last bright idea I ever had for nearly a month, but let's get back to the worst Christmas ever.

"Brendan! You were terrific!"

This came from my sister Sally. She's the family optimist.

"Thanks, Sal," I said.

Now that I had shed my Santa costume, I was donning my "brother" costume. Sally's husband, Arnie, stood behind her smiling the smile of a married man. I shook hands with the husbands, endured the cheek pecks from my sisters, then finally looked down at the swarming mass of children overrunning the compound of my feet. My sisters are Catholic. Need I say more? The oldest kid appeared to be about thirteen. He stood away from the rest of the toddlers and children with his hands in his pockets and a somber look on his face. Not sad or despairing, just somber, as if he had gone deaf two years ago, didn't know it, and was waiting for somebody to say something to him.

"What's your name?" I said, and Sally suddenly leaned in and said, "That's Steven, he's my oldest, he's thirteen and won a blue ribbon at a competition last summer at the Yentroc Championship Swimming Meet."

Steven glanced at his mother, then went back to looking somber. I got the picture so fast it left skid marks.

"What's popping, Steven?" I said, holding out my hand.

He glanced at his mother with what I interpreted as a nervous tic.

"Not much, Uncle Brendan," he said, shaking hands.

"Oh that's what he always says," Sally said. "He's shy around people, but don't let that fool you. Steven is a straight-A scholar, and last winter he had the lead role in the student production of *Carousel*. He played the same role that Gordon MacRae played in the movie, the role that Frank Sinatra walked away from leaving the cast high-and-dry. Don't you think that was a terrible thing to do to a group of young actors?"

I felt as if Dorothy had tossed a bucket of water—I was melting under this onslaught of uninteresting information. Steven glanced at his mom again, then glanced at me and shrugged. His hands went back into his pockets.

"I knew ye'd come through, boy-o," Maw said, elbowing her way toward me. She was beaming. Her son had managed to not embarrass the entire Murphy clan once again.

As an aside, let me tell you something about my Maw. When she's not around, she's as tall as Sister Mary Francis in my memory, so it's a shock to find myself looking down to see her face. I always remember looking up at her, usually from behind a chair or any other large object that might make it difficult for her to grab my ears. At the age of eight I discovered that the furnace in the basement was the best place to dodge her fingers—Maw was too matronly to squeeze behind the boiler.

"It's good to be home, Maw," I said.

"Did yeh get my note?" she said.

"I got your note, Maw," I said, and I saw the faintest trace of doubt in her eyes. "I didn't touch the liquor."

Note that I did not say "cabinet."

"Yer a good son, Brendan."

"I know."

"Round up yer banshees, daughters, it's time teh hit the road," Maw said. Her brogue always got thicker when referring to her beloved grandchildren. But then it also occurred when she was fit to be tied, so as with certain Latin words, you had to glean the meaning from the context. I failed Latin by the way.

"Maw," Gavin interjected at this point, "me and Brendan are going down to Duffy's for a quick one."

Maw turned on Gavin and squinted at him, then looked me up and down. "I've baked a blood pudding," she said. "It's warming in the oven."

"I know, Maw," Gavin replied. "Me and Brendan are going down to Duffy's for a quick one."

"Can yeh define 'quick'?" she said.

"We'll be home in an hour, Maw."

When Gavin and I were small children, me ol' Mither sometimes had trouble distinguishing him from me. We looked alike, we dressed alike, we spoke and walked and broke lamps alike. But by the age of twelve, Gavin had taken a different fork in the road. He had become an Eagle Scout, so my Maw had learned to trust him. I envied the power he wielded over her.

"I'll leave a platter of leftovers warming for my two truants," she said. I could tell she didn't really like trusting Gavin. She much preferred the certainty of mistrusting me.

The Murphy clan trooped out of the gymnasium and gathered on the sidewalk near the curb under the lightly falling snow. The various husbands went to get their cars. The children kept swarming. I felt like I was sinking into a sea of elves.

"I'm parked right here," Gavin said, pointing at a nearby rental car.

I was impressed, but not surprised, that he had found a parking space so close to the gymnasium door. Gavin and I were alike in many ways, and different in many ways, especially in the world of academic achievement. He understood baffling concepts such as "distance = speed × time," which I had been taught in algebra class and had found about as useful as a job résumé. But Gavin had an intuition concerning the practical application of mathematics. For example: How long does it take 2 brothers standing 23 feet from a car to escape the noise of 14 children? Answer: 11 seconds.

Distance = speed × time.

I never thought I would live to see an algebra formula save my sanity.

It was another Christmas miracle.

CHAPTER 12

"Are ya still driving a taxicab?" Gavin said, as he guided his rental away from the curb.

"Next question," I replied.

"Still writing?" he said, as he turned onto Douglas Avenue and headed toward the skyline of downtown Wichita.

I shifted uneasily on the shotgun seat. Shifting uneasily is one of the many writing techniques I had mastered over the years as an unpublished novelist. In fact, I had become so adept at it that few non-writers could detect its existence, like the hidden structure of a well-crafted novel. But Gavin wasn't one of them. He glanced at me as I shot a cough into my fist and cleared my throat. These are two techniques incorporated by genre authors. Authors of artistic litera-ture, on the other hand, are more subtle. Their uneasiness at being interrogated about the failure of their lifelong dreams to come true often consists of a quiet sniff and a sidelong glance of indifference in the opposite direction of the inquisitor. The end result is always the same though: Gavin chuckled.

"I suppose you heard about Tommy Malloy," he said.

Tommy Malloy was a boy we had known in high school. I looked over at Gavin. "No," I said. "Did he die or something?"

"He sold a suspense novel to Scribner's."

A jolt of electricity erupted from the car seat and traveled up my tailbone. It reminded me of the day Gavin and I went to see *The Tingler* (1959) at the Orpheum Theater in downtown Wichita. Our

row of seats had been wired to vibrate whenever the centipede mon-
ster appeared on screen. The movie was a William Castle production
of course, same as the *House on Haunted Hill,* where a cardboard
skeleton flew above the heads of the audience during the movie. Castle labeled this effect "Emerge-O." Wild teenagers hooted and tossed
popcorn at the skeleton. Between Vincent Price and the hoodlums,
Gavin and I were scared out of our wits. It was the best fifty cents
we ever spent.

"Is that right?" I said.

"That's right."

"I didn't know Malloy was trying to be a writer," I lied.

He glanced at me.

Damn.

"Been writing since high school from what his sister Beverly told
me," Gavin said, reaching into his shirt pocket and pulling out a
fresh toothpick. He slipped it between his grinning teeth. "I ran into
Beverly today at the Safeway. She said Tommy got a helluva big advance, too. Said he signed a contract for a three-book deal."

"Oh," I said. "A *commercial* writer, huh?"

"Is there any other kind?"

"James Joyce never made any money off his novels," I said.

"I believe it," he said.

I sensed he was baiting me. This was why I often referred to him
as my evil brother Gavin. This, and a thousand other irritating reasons. Gavin had never been impressed by my ambitions to become
a novelist. He was one of those squares who thought "maturity" was
the answer to all mankind's problems.

"Well ... good for Malloy," I said. "That just proves it can be
done. I'm glad for Tommy."

Gavin turned his head and looked right at me. His lips parted in a smile. He held the end of the toothpick between his tiny wolverine-like teeth and said, "Ya know something, kid. I believe ya."

He looked ahead at the snowflakes spiraling in the headlights as we made our way along Douglas Avenue, which was frosted white. There must have been an inch on the ground already. I hate snow. Unless I'm driving my cab. Then snow is my friend. People call cabs when it snows. Most urban drivers hate snow. My guess is that long-haul truck drivers hate snow, too, but I've never discussed the subject with a trucker. If I was a trucker, I would hate snow. These were the thoughts I had as we cruised toward Duffy's Pub. I was thinking these thoughts in order to take my mind off that dirty bastard Tommy Malloy and his goddamn three-book deal with Scribner's.

Duffy's Pub is a lot like Sweeney's Tavern back in Denver. Duffy knows Sweeney, but they haven't met in person. Sweeney sometimes calls Duffy when trying to track down my Maw in order to report my unruly behavior, usually on St. Patrick's Day.

Gavin and I walked into Duffy's Pub.

"Hey, the prodigal bum has returned!"

I recognized Duffy's voice right off. When I was seventeen I once tried to sneak into his pub. Duffy wasn't on the premises that night. The word on the street said that a recent graduate from a bartending school was on duty, so my high school buddies and I went in late to see if we could get away with buying a beer. Kid stuff, ya know? We were graduating seniors and the world was our oyster. A friend of mine named Mulligan looked "old" so we were going to grab a table in the back and let him do the ordering. We were wearing suits. We thought we were sly. Our pal Mulligan had prematurely gray hair, wore glasses like Buddy Holly, and could do an imitation of a harried businessman stopping off at a bar for a quick snort. He looked to be around thirty or so and knew the body language of the white-collar worker, the sighs, the sagging shoulders, the quick loosening of his tie as he raised a distracted finger and signaled for a drink. Bartenders rarely carded him. Some kids are born blessed. Mulligan sells insurance nowadays. He's a harried businessman.

To make a long story short, Duffy showed up about ten minutes after we got there and recognized me instantly. My father used to escort me into Duffy's Pub on Saturday afternoons after the Wichita Eagles baseball games. Duffy 86'd me for life. By "life" he meant until I turned twenty-one, but by that time I had fled Wichita.

"Driver's license, ya young hooligan," Duffy said, before Gavin and I even sat down on the stools. I removed my Colorado ID from my billfold.

Duffy took it in both hands and held it up to the flickering neon of a Budweiser sign. My heart was touched by that gesture. But then, instead of handing it back, he leaned both elbows on the bar and continued examining my license. "Forty-five years of age," he said.

I nodded.

"Six foot one," he said. I nodded.

"One hundred and ninety-two pounds," he said, and I stopped nodding.

He looked at my belly the way cops look at corpses.

He looked back at the license.

"Eyes ... blue. Sex ... male."

He stopped abruptly and looked me in the eye. "Where's yer corrective lenses, laddie?"

"I wear contacts," I said.

"Contacts?"

"Disposable contact lenses," I said.

"*Disposable!*" he said. "Did yeh hit the lottery, King Midas?"

"No. The disposability factor makes them inexpensive purchase items," I said. "Especially if you never dispose of them."

"A chip off the ol' block," he said, and handed the license back. "Have a seat, young Brendan Murphy."

Gavin and I started to slip onto two vacant barstools, but suddenly I stopped. I saw someone at the rear of the bar, seated in the same booth where Mulligan and my pals once tried to violate the liquor laws of the sovereign State of Kansas. It was a Santa Claus. Fer the luvva Christ, I was seeing them everywhere.

"What'll it be then, eh?" Duffy said.

We settled onto our stools. Gavin ordered two draughts.

After Duffy set them in front of us, I indicated the far corner of the bar with my thumb. "Is Santa off-duty?" I said.

Duffy glanced at the booth, then frowned.

"A painful case, that one," he said. He picked up a rag and began wiping the bar.

"How so?" I said.

"This evening at six o'clock his job came to an end. He's unemployed now."

"Who is he?" I said.

Duffy raised his chin. "That forlorn fellow happens to be the ..." He stopped and glanced at me. "I believe you know him. That's the Callahan boy ... Jimmy. You went to school with him, did you not?"

I nearly choked. Jimmy *Callahan!*

Choking is something I do whenever I encounter a high school acquaintance.

I nodded. "Yeah. He was a fullback or something on the baseball team."

Gavin snickered and shook his head in disgust. "Callahan was the captain, as well as the center, of your senior varsity basketball team," he said pedantically. "He made all-state."

I nodded quickly and kept on nodding to imply that my brain already contained those facts and he wasn't revealing anything new to me, which he was.

What's a center?

I stopped nodding and peered at Gavin. I thought about telling him my Dyna-Plex Christmas story just to change the subject, but then I decided not to. He was the kind of person to whom you didn't tell certain embarrassing things. He was my brother.

"What's this story Maw told me about you playing a Santa Claus at Dyna-Plex?" Gavin said.

Fer the luvva Christ.

"I was just helping a fellow out is all," I said.

"Say, how come you quit that typing job at Dyna-Plex?" Gavin said. "You were making good money according to Maw."

Maw and her letters to everybody. Suddenly I wondered if she ever mentioned Sweeney when she wrote to my siblings.

"I quit because I couldn't stand it anymore," I said.

"The way Maw told it, I got the impression that you were working as a Santa Claus for the entire holiday season like your pathetic buddy over there."

"He was never my buddy," I said. "I didn't play basketball in high school, as you well know."

"Saints be praised," Gavin said.

Gavin had been an athlete in high school. Football. Basketball. Baseball. Track. Eagle Scout. Altar boy. Do-gooder. Homework hand-inner on time. Again, we differ in some respects.

"Maybe I'll go over and say hi to Callahan," I said.

"Why?" Gavin replied. "He's not your buddy."

I looked Gavin in the eye. "Once a Santa, always a Santa. That makes Jimmy my buddy. You would understand if you had served in the army."

Gavin's face froze. He had never quite gotten over the fact that I had done something strenuous that he had never done. That made two of us.

I slipped off the stool and carried my beer over to the table where Callahan was staring at his half-empty glass. The symbolism was too much to bear. I signaled Duffy for two more draughts.

I looked down at Santa.

"Callahan," I said.

He looked up at me with somewhat dull eyes.

"Remember me?" I said.

"No."

"Brendan Murphy," I said. "Does that ring a bell?"

"No."

"We attended grade school and high school together."

"No."

"You played on the varsity basketball team and I was a ... a ... I was in your chemistry class."

"No."

This might have gone on forever, but Duffy showed up with the beers and set them on the table.

Then I realized what I was doing wrong. I was trying to "make normal conversation." Doubtless it was because I was in another city, out of my element, and I wasn't seated behind the steering wheel of my taxicab. Since I have absolutely no social skills whatsoever, I realized I had to shift gears and do what I do best: pretend.

Physically, I slipped into the booth and pushed one of the beers across the table toward Callahan. Mentally, I started my engine, dropped my flag, and turned on my meter. Suddenly I was seated in Rocky Mountain Taxicab #123.

"This one's on me, pal," I said. "I'm not surprised you don't remember me since I am probably the least-remembered student in our graduating class. But I remember everybody, and as I recall you were the only player on the varsity basketball team to make all-state."

I saw a change come into his eyes. It's a funny thing about eyes. They're the most expressive parts of the human body in non-violent situations. I see a lot of eyes in my rearview mirror when I'm driving my taxi—in fact I see very little else since mirrors aren't that big, although I do quite a bit of mirror-adjusting when a beautiful woman climbs into my backseat, but let's move on. Callahan's eyes told me that I had triggered something inside him. He squinted at me and said, "Aren't you the kid who stood on top of your desk in sixth grade?"

CHAPTER 13

"Yeah," I admitted.

"Man, we thought the nun was gonna kill you."

"That makes two of us."

"Do you remember Annie Burke and Katy Oberman?" he said.

"Sure," I said.

"After the nun dragged you into the hall, they got down on their knees and started praying."

"For what?"

"Your salvation."

"If you ever run into them, tell them I said thanks. I think it worked."

Annie Burke and Katy Oberman—wow, I hadn't thought about them in years. They were the holiest girls at BVP. On Halloween they dressed like flying nuns.

"Whatever became of Annie and Katy?" I said.

"After high school they joined a commune and blew their minds on acid."

"So what have you been up to since high school?" I said.

That was the wrong thing to say. The dullness came back into his eyes. He picked up his half-empty beer and drained it. He set it back down and looked at me. "Oh, you know … this and that."

"Me too," I said. "Right now I drive a taxi in Denver."

"You made it all the way to Denver, huh?" he said. I wasn't sure what he meant by that but I "went with the flow."

"Yep," I said. "After I got out of the army I went to KAU for a couple of years, then I moved to Atlanta. I kind of bummed around the country working day jobs. I've been to L.A., San Francisco, Cleveland. I was in Philadelphia twice but that was by accident."

"You served in the army?" he said.

"Well … that depends on your definition of 'serve.'"

He nodded. He picked up his fresh beer and took a sip. I got the message. He didn't want to talk. I'm so used to tuning people out that I have to make an attitude adjustment when I find myself in the presence of a "dead battery," as we cabbies say. Silence can be unnerving in a taxi, so I always try to get people to talk about themselves during a ride. This allows me to think about more interesting things, although I am required to nod my head in apparent agreement every thirty seconds. I don't mind, because the physical act of nodding keeps me awake. When you drive a taxi for a living, the number-one rule is "Safety First."

"I hope you don't mind my asking," I said, "but why are you wearing a Santa Claus suit?"

"I've been working as a Santa for the past couple weeks," Callahan said. "I've been trying to pick up some extra money."

"Extra money?" I said. "What's that?"

He raised his chin and peered at me. "You know. Just … money," he said.

I shouldn't have asked that, but he caught me off guard. To me, "extra" money is like "spending" money. It's only money in the way that "cellulite" is only fat, ladies. But I quickly reminded myself that not everybody thinks like I do. I have never had the sense that I am on anybody else's wavelength. In fact, I'm not even sure I have a wavelength.

"I just thought you meant on top of your regular job," I said, trying to sound logical in order to cover up my *faux pas*, a move that I have not completely mastered, although I am getting better at it with the passage of time. I calculate that by the time I'm dead, I'll be a pro.

"I don't have a regular job," Callahan said. "My Santa job ended today. I pulled two hours at a department store downtown. Now it's over."

It always raises my spirits to hear that someone no longer has a job, but I could tell by Callahan's demeanor that he was normal.

"What are you going to do now?" I said.

"I don't know. I've never had a job that lasted very long, but I always find something. I stay busy. I'll have to find something soon though, I guess."

I picked up my beer and took a quick sip to stifle my joy. His remark took me back to Pittsburgh where I had lived for six months on unemployment benefits. I still think of Pittsburgh as "Eden."

I set my beer down and said, "This is a funny coincidence, but I pulled a couple of Santa Claus gigs this season, too."

"Really?" he said, looking at me with the same doubtful expression that most people employ when I talk.

"One hour ago I was wearing a Santa Claus costume just like yours," I said. That sounded like such a line of bull that I quickly told him about my BVP performance.

When I finished, Callahan started weeping.

I froze.

"What's the matter, buddy?" I said, shifting into overdrive. I've had weepers in the backseat of my taxi so I know how to negotiate tears—the Dead Man's Curve of cab driving.

Callahan wiped his eyes with his beard and looked at me. "I'm sorry, Brendan, but ..."

"Please … call me Murph," I said, without explanation.

"I'm sorry, Murph, it's just that … Mister Olsen hasn't made it to the Christmas pageant once in the past five years. So I got in touch with Monsignor O'Leary and asked if I could have the job this evening, but he …"

"Wait a minute … hold on," I said, raising my right palm. "What do you mean *job*? Are you saying this was a paying gig?"

"Fifty bucks," Callahan said. "But Monsignor …"

"Wait a minute … wait a minute … the parish pays the Santa Claus fifty bucks to do that?"

"Yes, but …"

"Cash?"

"Yes." He didn't go on. He waited for me to interrupt him again, but I didn't. The word "cash" had brought me to a screeching halt.

"But Monsignor O'Leary wouldn't let me do it," he finished.

"Why not?"

Callahan raised his beer glass and looked at me through the golden bubbles. "I've got a reputation," he said. Then he tilted the glass to his mouth and drained it off.

Fer the luvva Christ.

Another drunk Santa.

I couldn't believe it. This former all-state basketball champion of Blessed Virgin Catholic High School had become a living cliché. Suddenly I didn't feel so alone.

"He was afraid I might show up drunk," Callahan said. "We Santas live in a goldfish bowl. The Word gets out."

I looked at my wristwatch. Gavin and I were due home in half an hour, which meant we had to leave in fifteen minutes in order to get there in time for Gavin to demonstrate once again what a reliable bastard he was. I felt like I was driving #123. I felt like a quarterback working the clock, making judicious decisions as the precious seconds ticked away. I had an unemployed man on my hands, and unless I worked fast he might be looking for a job soon. I had to stop him. I had to make him realize that there are worse things in life than being unemployed—like being employed.

"You must have made out fairly well if you worked the holiday season," I said.

"I did okay," he said.

This was a delicate moment. I wanted to know exactly how much money he had. His future joblessness depended on it. But you don't ask an American how much money he has. It doesn't matter about his race or ethnic background or religion or what part of the country he grew up in or what side of the track he lives on or how much education he has. All that matters is how much moola he has in his pocket. "Moola"—from the caveman word "*Moog*"—meaning "moneygrubber."

"I was talking to a Santa just last week," I said in an offhand tone of voice, "and he told me that a hard-working guy could rake in six grand during the holiday season. That's in Denver, of course, where everything is relatively cheap. What's it like here in Wichita?"

Callahan shrugged. "About the same."

"Wow, you must have made out like a bandit," I said, trying to sound naive and tactless. This didn't take any effort.

"Naw. I only earned two grand."

I made some quick calculations. Two grand could carry a man a long way on the mean streets of Denver.

"Well hell, you probably don't need to start looking for work until after the new year," I said. "Or even February."

He gazed at me with a familiar expression of incomprehensibility. "I don't think two grand would last that long," he said.

I gritted my teeth and rubbed my face with both hands. Again, I had to remind myself that nobody else thinks like I do. I once lived for a year on two grand, although I realize that inflation has been adjusted a few times since then. But it was the principle of the thing: anybody who has two thousand dollars simply has no business working—bottom line.

I started to feel helpless. They say that a man has to want to quit before he can stop working, that nobody can stop working for him. His first step is to make a fearless inventory of his life and admit to himself that he has a job.

But I held out one small hope for Callahan: right at that moment he was in between jobs. He was clean and drunk. If I could just convince him to hold onto this ray of hope, I might save him from heading down the wrong path, at least until February. By then he might have recovered to the point where he could handle cab driving.

"Hey come on, Callahan," I said. "It's Christmas. Why ruin it? I say don't even think about a job until after the new year. Give yourself a break, ya know what I mean? Hell, back in Denver I take a week off every month just to unwind. I call it my monthly spring break."

Note that I did not mention cab driving right then. I was toying with him, but not in a bad way. I was toying with him in the way that an expert fisherman will play a trout where the water runs deep. Maybe a better way to put it is that I was trying to plant an idea in his head through the power of subliminal suggestion. Or perhaps a better way is to say that I was practicing *mind control!!!* I wanted the poor bastard to become a cabbie. I wanted him to never work again as long as he lived. I want this for all Americans.

"Partners in crime," a voice said.

I looked up. Gavin was standing by the table holding a beer mug.

"Nice suit, Callahan," Gavin said. "Red is your color."

Gavin had been one year ahead of us in high school, so he could get away with saying stuff like that. When I was a kid I hated upperclassmen. I still do.

"Hello, Gavin," Callahan said.

I looked at Callahan with surprise. "You remember my brother?"

"Sure," Callahan said. "He was a year ahead of us in school. And he was an Eagle Scout."

All of the sudden I didn't feel like helping Callahan. He had been a Boy Scout in our troop. He had even gone to Camp Wa-Ni-Ta-Ka the same summer I found ten dollars in a boat—there's more to that story, but let's move on. Gavin wasn't with us though. He had been chosen by the scoutmasters to attend a national Boy Scout Jamboree in Maryland. They paid his bus fare. He won a big deal knot-tying contest and came home with a medal. I don't want to talk about it.

"We better hit the road, Brendan," Gavin said.

I glanced at my wristwatch. A quarter till. Time was up. I looked at Jimmy Callahan and my heart went out to him, even though he remembered my brother but not me. I don't know why it would bother me not to be recognized. I hate it when anybody recognizes me on the mean streets of Denver, whether old acquaintances or old taxi fares. I live for anonymity. It's the next best thing to fame.

"I gotta run, pal," I said to him. "Think about what I said, okay? Promise me you won't do anything crazy, like look for a job. Give yourself a week to dry out." I reached into my billfold and pulled out a Rocky Mountain Taxicab receipt, a 2x3-inch card, and scribbled my Maw's number on it. "If you get the urge to work before the new year, call me. I'll talk you down."

Callahan took the card and studied it, then he looked up at me. "Thanks, Murph. I promise I'll think about it."

"Thinking is all I ever ask of anybody," I said with a smile. I'm usually disappointed. I wished him a Merry Christmas, then I walked toward the exit where I wished Duffy a Merry Christmas.

Duffy asked if I would be in town for the New Year's celebration at his pub. I told him no, that I would be celebrating at Sweeney's.

"Glad to hear it," Duffy said. "He'll call me instead of me calling him to report your unruly behavior."

I hurried out the door with Gavin at my back.

"What did Duffy mean by that?" Gavin said.

"Ya got me."

"And what was that 'Murph' stuff with Callahan?"

"Back in Denver my friends call me 'Murph,'" I said.

"Did you tell Callahan to call you 'Murph'?"

"I might have hinted at it."

Gavin snickered and climbed into the driver's seat. I climbed in shotgun and sat back, pondering the fact that Gavin was really starting to get on my nerves.

CHAPTER 14

We drove the silent streets of Wichita. There were at least two inches of snow on the road. Not much traffic. We passed a Yellow Cab. This made me think of Callahan. I once made a vow to myself—well, once is lowballing it—to never get involved in the personal lives of my taxi fares. It seemed like every time I took an interest in the life of a stranger and tried to help, things took a nosedive. That was Step 1 in the process. Step 2 consisted of me trying to fix the mess I had made. When I was in fourth grade the nun once asked us if we knew any words that were pronounced like "medal" but were spelled differently. I raised my hand. I was the only kid in class who was familiar with the word "meddle."

"What does 'meddle' mean, Brendan?" the nun said.

"It means to mess around with things you shouldn't."

She nodded her approval. I guess it was approval. Maybe it was confirmation.

Yet there I was, getting involved in the life of a person who wasn't even a taxi fare. But he was a guy who had a problem I could easily fix. The solution was cab driving. The solution to all mankind's problems is cab driving, but try and tell that to the Pentagon.

I guess I was sort of like a person who has seen a really great movie or read a really great book and then ran around trying to get his friends to read it. You're bursting to let everyone know that they should take some time to enrich their lives. Why I think their lives will be enriched if they listen to me, I don't know. Maybe it's my ego.

But when I see someone like Callahan, it's like seeing a car parked at the side of the road with its hood raised. If you're even half a man, you get the urge to help. That's my excuse anyway.

I suppose I'm something of a proselytizer. I feel like a chosen individual to whom The Truth has been revealed. Ironically, I get guys like that in my taxi every week and most of them are a pain in the neck. But I have to agree with everything The Doomsday Prophets say if I expect a tip. According to a little notebook I keep, the world is going to end on seventeen different dates within the next three years. I've got my fingers crossed.

"Well, here we are 'Murph,'" Gavin said, as he parked his rental in front of the ol' homestead.

I realized that I shouldn't have told Callahan to call me "Murph." I had forgotten that, technically speaking, every member of my family is a "Murph."

"In the future you can leave the quotes off my nickname," I said. "If that's too much trouble, I can always rub your face in the snow. They taught me judo in the army, you know."

That shut him up. The army was a sore point with Gavin, but I almost never brought up the subject because he still possessed one more medal than I did. In the army they never gave you medals for pushing mops, but they did punish you for not doing things right. That didn't seem quite fair to me.

We climbed out of the car and headed up the sidewalk. The lights were on inside the house, but the shades were drawn. The snow had been considerably trampled, so I stopped to examine the footprints, particularly those of the children. I noted with satisfaction that the freshest footprints headed *away* from the house. Basil Rathbone is my favorite detective.

When we got up to the porch I told Gavin to wait a moment, then I leaned toward the door and listened.

"What are you doing? he said.

"Reliving my childhood."

No sounds from the house. I grasped the doorknob, turned it clockwise, and pushed the door open. Still no sounds.

"The coast is clear," I said, and somehow Gavin seemed to understand what I meant.

We stepped inside and were immediately engulfed by the odor of blood pudding. I glanced at Gavin and saw that he was already glancing at me. Neither Gavin nor I had ever eaten blood pudding. From the ages of approximately four to eighteen we had been served blood pudding every Christmas, yet neither of us knew what blood pudding tasted like. By the looks in our eyes I could tell we both planned to keep it that way. Only problem? Shelteen had passed away long ago and there was no dog to slip the food to.

I heard the clank of dishes coming from the kitchen. Maw was cleaning up. I didn't know this for a fact, but I believed that when Maw was a new bride she had taken a vow never to go to bed while a dirty dish remained within one hundred yards of her sink. This had irritated me, even eluded me, but I guess some of it rubbed off on me, because I always do the dish whenever I finish a burger. Cleaning up after lunch consists of wadding a delicatessen wrapper and tossing it into a trash barrel.

"We're home!" I yelled.

"Jaysus," Gavin said irritably.

When I was a kid I always yelled when I came home. I had seen kids do this on TV and I wanted to be like them. To a certain extent I suppose you could say I succeeded.

Maw came out of the kitchen drying her hands with a towel. Her eyes were twinkling. "There they are," she said. "Me two young hoodlums."

"Aw Maw," I said.

"Yeh missed the family party," she said.

"Darn," I grumbled.

I tried not to look at Gavin. He knew what a fraud I was. We were brothers, ergo I had always made a special point of never living in the same city as him.

"The girls have gone back to the hotel with the children," she said. I noticed that she didn't mention the husbands. I liked that.

"Where are they staying? I said.

"The downtown Holiday."

My heart stopped. That's where I had rented a room. I started making quick calculations. If I returned to the Holiday, the odds were fair that I might run into a relative either tonight or tomorrow morning. My brain went *boing*. I knew I would be sleeping in my old bedroom that night. I had originally intended to hitch a ride with Gavin back to the hotel after we figured out how to clean our plates without actually eating anything.

"I've got yer blood pudding warming in the oven," Maw said. "Take off yer coats and have a seat at the kitchen table."

As she walked back into the kitchen I looked at Gavin with horror in my eyes. "What are we going to *do*?" I said plaintively.

He removed the toothpick from between his teeth. The wood was cracked in two. "Kid," he said, "I think we've reached the end of the line. We're gonna have to eat it."

"Come on, Gavin," I whined, "you were an Eagle Scout. Get us out of this."

"You were a *soldier*," Gavin said. "Weren't you trained in escape and evasion?"

"I was on sick-call that day."

We hung our coats in the closet and trudged into the kitchen. In desperation, I began whistling "When Irish eyes are smiling ..."

"Shelteen is dead," Gavin muttered.

"Yeah, but maybe ..."

"Give it up, kid."

Maw was already scooping the reheated blood pudding onto our plates. As Gavin and I sat down, Maw stood back and folded her arms. "Well, yer both grown men now," she said, "so I suppose yeh'd prefer beer over glasses of good healthy milk."

Even though Albert Einstein claimed to have disproven the theory of simultaneity, Gavin and I said yes at the exact same time. I love debunking science.

"I believe I'll join yeh," she said.

She went to the fridge and brought out three bottles of Guinness Stout. I had never cared much for the taste of stout, but I knew I would need something stronger than Miller Light to endure this crucible.

Since our ol' Dad was no longer with us, I volunteered to do the honors. I popped the caps off the bottles with a church key that was so old it had rust spots. It was the same church key I had used as a kid to pop soda bottle tops.

"How about I buy you a new bottle opener for Christmas, Maw?" I said.

"Yer father gave me this church key on our first wedding anniversary," she said, snatching it from my grasp.

Nuff said.

Gavin raised his bottle. "Merry Christmas, Maw."

She raised her bottle and I raised mine. We clanked them together. Like handshaking, bottle clanking is another facet of Murphy
get-togethers. If it wasn't for the presence of the blood pudding, this
might have been a magical moment.

"Dig in," Maw said, pointing at our plates.

If you don't know what blood pudding is, do what me ol' Dad
used to tell me to do: "Look it up in the dictionary, laddie." If you
do that you might find yourself also looking up "suet" as well as "tallow." I don't want to ruin your research fun but "tallow" is related to
the production of soap.

I glanced at the door to the basement. It was adjacent to the
refrigerator. I wondered if somehow, by some surreptitious means,
we might be able to use the door in a last desperate attempt to dispose of the food without eating it. It would take nerves of steel and
split-second timing. One of us would have to concoct an impec-
cable diversionary tactic worthy of Rommel to distract Maw while
the other dashed to the door, tossed the pudding downstairs, and
slipped back to the table. I looked at Gavin, then looked at the door,
then looked at Gavin. He saw what I was thinking. He could read
me like an X-ray.

"Give it up, kid," he mumbled.

I shrugged and placed the first spoonful of blood pudding—ever
in my life—on my tongue and simultaneously drove the neck of
the stout toward my lips. But then I held off. I rolled the pudding
around in my mouth, then swallowed it and looked at Gavin. "Say,
this isn't half bad," I said.

Gavin nodded at me as he masticated with his lips clamped
tight. He swallowed his first spoonful of blood pudding ever in his
life and said, "Not bad at all."

"What do yeh mean by that?" Maw said.

We froze.

"Yer acting as if ye'd never tasted my pudding in yer lives," she said.

I glanced at Gavin. His eyes drilled into mine, looking for answers that didn't exist. Fer the luvva Christ, I was forty-five years old, yet I felt like a ten-year-old boy caught peeking at a girly magazine. Remind me to tell you my girly magazine story sometime.

There was only one thing to do: lie.

"I haven't tasted anything this good since I left home, Maw." This is my favorite type of lie: the irrelevant lie. In fact, I had tasted better foods than blood pudding since I left home, but it had no relevance to the question concerning her pudding, which was actually good, made from the blood of what is known in advertising circles as "the other white meat," i.e., pork, pig, hog, swine, etc.

"How about before you left home, boy-o?" she said.

"Pardon me, mother?" I said, raising a second spoonful to my lips. Gavin's mouth was hard at work avoiding conversation.

"Is this blood pudding as good as the blood pudding I made before yeh went out into the world teh seek yer fortune?" Maw said.

"Why yes," I said, and shoved it in.

"How would yeh know that, since yeh spent the faarst eighteen years of yer life feeding yer blood pudding to poor little Shelteen?"

Gavin stopped eating and hung his head with shame. I set my spoon on my plate and gazed at Maw.

"Is that what killed her?" I said.

"No," Maw said. "According to the vet, Shelteen passed away from an overdose of Alpo."

I nodded. "Well, I guess that was back in the days before people knew that dog food was bad for dogs."

"I was onto the both of ye hoodlums from the outset," Maw said, smiling one of those thin-lipped victorious smiles that mothers display when they know they've got their sons by the short hairs. "Always afraid of trying something new, weren't yeh?"

This was true. In this way, I feel I was a typical American kid. But it didn't apply just to the fear of eating new types of food. Whenever chicken gravy seeped into the peas on my plate during Sunday dinner, I freaked out. When Maw bought Skippy peanut butter instead of Peter Pan, I sulked for days. The first time she set a plate of liver and onions in front of me, I went into cardiac arrest. I never did forgive her for bringing home that lime sherbet.

And I never will.

"But Maw," I said, "if you knew we were secretly giving our blood pudding to Shelteen, why didn't you berate us vociferously?"

"Aaah Brendan," she said with a sigh. "If I berated you every time you got up to your shenanigans, it would have sent me to an early grave. Like the time yeh stood on yer desk at school, it was either box yer ears or pretend yeh were the next-door neighbor's son."

"You pretended I was Danny *Mulvehill*?"

"That I did, that I did."

"Aw Maw, I'm sorry I made you pretend that."

Danny Mulvehill was the ruffian who had taught me how to cross the street by myself when I was four years old. He's currently pulling a nickel in Leavenworth.

"I forgive yeh," Maw said. "Yer a good son."

"I know."

"What about me?" Gavin said, looking back-and-forth at us during our "clearing of the air."

"Yer the best son," Maw said. "As far as I know, feeding Shelteen yer blood pudding was the only bad thing you ever did."

"What about that kitchen chair?" I said.

Gavin kicked me under the table. It brought me back to reality. I felt as if I was coming out of a dream. I had the goods on Gavin, goods going clear back to the age of three when he used to steal lollipops from me. I had so many goods on him that I could have destroyed Maw's fraudulent image of him right then and there.

But I decided to clam up.

I wasn't going to destroy Gavin. No ... not tonight. It was the night before Christmas Eve, and the entire family would be gathering for a big dinner the next afternoon, including uncles, aunts, cousins, and handshakers from all over the country. No. I would not destroy Gavin tonight. I would bide my time. I would wait like a spider crouched in the center of a web, patiently watching a fly buzzing around the room. And then ... when the fly landed on a single sticky strand ... I would slowly crawl toward ...

"Got any more blood pudding?" Gavin said, interrupting the most ludicrous fantasy I had indulged in since the day I dropped my first novel into a mailbox.

CHAPTER 15

"Tell me, Brendan, have yeh finished yer Christmas shopping?" Maw said, as Gavin and I helped her clear the table for the last do of the night.

"'Finished' isn't the word," I said. "I haven't even started yet."

"Yeh put it off until the last minute again, eh?" Maw said. "Just like yer homework when yeh were in college."

"Aw Maw, I never did homework in college. You're thinking of grade school. I plan to take care of it tomorrow."

"The stores close at six o'clock in the evening," she said.

"I know, I know, don't worry, Maw, I got it under control."

"Yeh needn't buy presents for every blessed relative," she said.

I liked that.

"I know, Maw. I never buy presents for anybody I don't have to."

"I always told the good sisters at Blessed Virgin that yeh were smarter than yeh looked, boy-o."

"Thanks, Maw," I said. Then I paused a moment. "Say Maw?"

"What is it, Brendan?"

"I ran into Jimmy Callahan this evening at Duffy's Pub."

"Did yeh now?"

"Yeah."

She smiled and said, "Did yeh say hello to Duffy for me?"

"Oh sure. But the reason I bring it up is that Jimmy told me that Mister Olsen hasn't played Santa Claus at the parish pageant for the past five years."

"A painful case, that Mister Olsen," Maw said, drying her hands on a towel.

"But the thing is," I continued unabatedly, "Jimmy told me that he applied for the Santa job but Monsignor O'Leary turned him down ..."

Maw's hands slowed on the towel.

"... because Jimmy apparently has a drinking problem and ..."

Slower and slower writhed my mother's hands.

"... so Jimmy wasn't able to play Santa this year," I said, but my voice had begun to wither. My mother's hands stopped moving. The towel was now gripped tightly in her fists.

Were the two of us in total mother/son synch at that moment on that night in Wichita? All I know is, I suddenly didn't feel like bringing up the subject of the fifty-dollar fee that a Santa Claus got paid to pinch-hit for Mister Olsen. I looked Maw in the eye. I became uneasy. Have you ever seen Mount Rushmore? The George Washington part I mean? The way George seems to stare without moving? I know that's just an illusion, but my mother held an eerie resemblance to the father of our country right at that moment.

I glanced at Gavin.

He seemed to sense "the vibe" even though he hadn't heard Jimmy mention the fee back at Duffy's. I didn't see fear in Gavin's eyes, but I did see something like a nervous runner crouched at a starting line waiting for the crack of a pistol.

Maw spoke softly: "What are yeh getting at?"

Her hands began moving again, wringing the damp towel, twisting and squeezing until something that might have been blood dripped to the floor if it had been red instead of clear.

"I told Jimmy that I ended up playing Santa for Mister Olsen this year and he couldn't believe the irony of the whole situation," I said with a grin. "We sure had a good laugh over that one."

Maw began nodding. The towel stopped dripping. "Yeh always were the one with the sense of humor, Brendan."

"It's probably time for me to go," Gavin said.

I looked at him in panic. What to do? Stay here with this woman who had robbed me of fifty dollars or go to the downtown Holiday and risk talking to a relative? The answer came in a flash: I would pay a *hundred* dollars to avoid a relative.

"Thanks for the drinks at Duffy's," I said to Gavin. "And thanks for the ride over here. Are you sure you don't want to spend the night in your old bedroom?"

"I've got a room at the Holiday," he said.

"No kidding?" I said. I laughed heartily and helped him on with his coat. "Yeh have yerself a good night's sleep, Gavin me boy," I said, mocking me ol' Mither's brogue while simultaneously slapping Gavin on the back and guiding him gently toward the front door. He gave me a "funny" look. This I was used to.

As soon as I locked the door, me ol' Mither said, "Be a good son and carry out the trash for me, will yeh Brendan?"

"Okay, Maw—but that will have to be your Christmas gift for this year."

She laughed. You would be surprised at how many people wouldn't laugh at a joke like that. Americans are incredibly touchy about free things.

I grabbed two full trash bags and carried them out the back door. Trash bags are among my favorite consumer products. I wish I had invented them. What a racket. People buy them, take them home, and throw them away. Let's see Bill Gates top that.

I felt an authentic rush of nostalgia as I gazed at the ol' backyard. Three inches of snow covered the vast quarter-acre of dirt. The Tarzan tree was still there, stripped of its leaves. At the back of the yard where the sidewalk ended stood an ancient barbecue pit that we Murphys had never used, as had so many Americans during the 1950s when it was both fun and legal to fill the skies with carcinogens. When I was a tot, I asked my Maw why we didn't hold barbecues on Sundays like other people, and she told me that the odor tended to draw neighbors.

I stood for a moment on the sidewalk and looked at the pristine perfection of the snow covering the backyard. Then I began moving forward with my feet planted flat on the sidewalk. I didn't lift my feet, I slid them, drilling the snow aside. I gritted my teeth and made a "grunn, grunn" sound. I was playing "snowplow." Nobody could see me. But suddenly I stopped. What if Gavin was watching? What if he hadn't gone to the hotel?

Damn.

I glanced around at the corners of the house expecting to see his grinning phiz peeking at me, but he wasn't there. I was alone. Just as I had been alone on that hot summer night thirty-five years earlier when I held a "secret" barbecue in our backyard.

All right. Here's my girly magazine story:

I was sitting at the soda fountain at a Rexall drugstore drowning my sorrows in a chocolate sundae. I was ten. I was leafing through a magazine called *Dolce,* which consisted of action photographs taken from cities around the world, combined with brief paragraphs describing the obvious. I had grabbed it off the rack after I slouched into the drugstore. I did this all the time, reading and sipping sodas and never paying for the magazines that I wrinkled. The soda jerk didn't seem to mind, and the pharmacist was a hundred years old. I turned a page and there was a stripper. She was working a Berlin nightclub. A python was draped around her shoulders. I studied the snake with scientific curiosity for a while, then decided that this magazine could act as a supplement to the science textbook we used in school. I might even be able to apply the knowledge I learned about snakes to improve my overall grade average. The magazine cost a quarter, so it seemed to me that a German biology textbook would be a much better investment than another chocolate sundae.

After I got it home, I immediately became worried. What if my Maw found this textbook and inquired about my sudden interest in the *Pythonidae* branch of the reptile family. I hadn't yet learned how to plan my surreptitious moves. That would come with time. But I realized I was doomed.

You couldn't hide anything from my Maw. She once found a three-inch diameter ball of used Juicy Fruit chewing gum that I had hidden in the back of my chest of drawers next to an overdue library book. She demanded to know why I was saving chewing gum. Cripes, did she really expect an explanation? There wasn't any explanation. Sometimes I think mothers are out of touch with reality.

But back to the hula girl. I decided there was only one way out of this inextricable mess. I would have to burn the magazine.

I was somewhat incorrect when I told you I hadn't yet learned how to plan my surreptitious moves. More precisely, I hadn't learned how to plan them *well*. I should have simply gone next door and tossed the magazine into the Mulvehill's garbage can. But no. Instead, I waited until nightfall then slipped into the pitch-black backyard on that hot August night carrying a box of wooden matchsticks.

I stood with my back to the kitchen door hiding my surreptitious moves from view. I removed the magazine from inside my shirt and placed it on the grill. I struck a match and held it to the cover of the magazine, and the backyard was suddenly flooded with a light so blinding that Gus could have seen it from outer space.

Wellsir, I started hammering the flaming magazine with my tiny fists. That didn't work, so I picked up a log and pounded on the pages, scattering ashes all the hell over the backyard, trying to dim the light before my Maw glanced out the kitchen window and dragged me off to confession.

But I did it. The light went out and the half-burned magazine lay smoldering on the grill. I panicked. I picked it up and stuffed it into my shirt. I didn't get any blisters on my chest, but the hot pages did serve to underscore my problem with planning.

I casually strolled up to the kitchen door and pulled it open and stepped inside. I decided to hide the remains of the magazine under my mattress until I could figure my next move. Maw was doing the dishes. As soon as I walked in, she took one sniff and said, "Is something burning?"

"No."

"Are yeh playing with matches again, yeh little scamp?"

"No."

"Are yeh telling yer tired old mother the truth?"

"Yes."

She was in her late thirties at the time, but that's neither here nor there.

It was only then that I realized the magazine was probably making an unsightly bulge in my little short-sleeved Madras shirt, but she didn't seem to notice. She was too busy searching my eyes for the truth, of all places.

I sidled past her and went upstairs to my room. The story more or less ends there. The next day I carried the burned wreckage all the way to the Rexall and tossed it into their dumpster. A superfluous journey, Mulvehillwise, but at least I was making progress in the planning department. I spent the rest of the afternoon drowning my sorrows in sundaes and reading *Daffy Duck* comics. I was quits with photojournalism.

I set the two trash bags in the snow next to the gate that led to the alley, then I turned and snowplowed back toward the house, glancing at The Tree, The Tree!

When I got back inside the house the phone was ringing.

"Can yeh pick that up, boy-o?" Maw said.

I gritted my teeth.

This was a trick Maw had been playing on me since I was seven. If I was living at home, I was the one who had to answer the telephone. She was always conveniently beating rugs or watching TV. I was onto her.

"Hello?"

"Brendan?"

It was like a knife in my heart. I didn't recognize the voice. Who the hell knew I was here?

"This is Duffy," he said.

I calmed down. A call from a bartender always has this effect.

"What can I do for you, Mister Duffy?"

"Come and get your friend Jimmy Callahan."

"What?"

"He's drunk and getting out of hand. Five minutes ago he applied for a job as a busboy. I told him I don't use busboys. He started weeping, then he asked me to call you. He needs a ride home."

Fer the luvva Christ. This was the price I paid for getting involved in someone's personal life. Jimmy Callahan wasn't a taxi fare and I wasn't on duty, but like cops and messiahs, asphalt warriors are on-call twenty-four hours a day.

"I'll be right there," I said. I hung up.

"Who was that?" Maw said. She was watching a *Perry Mason* rerun. When I was a kid I didn't like *Perry Mason*. Too much talk and not enough gunplay. Nothing's changed.

"Maw, can I borrow your car? Duffy asked me to come to the pub and take Jimmy Callahan home."

"Is he busting up the joint?"

"Worse. He's looking for a job."

"The keys are in my purse."

I gritted my teeth. "Could you please get them for me, Maw? I'm afraid of women's purses."

"Ach," she said, getting up and going to the closet. Some things don't have to be explained to my Maw, and I'm one of them.

I went out to the garage where the car was parked. My Maw owns a 1954 Buick Special in perfect running condition. It's fire-engine red like the doors to my 1963 Chevy back in Denver. The rest of my car is black. It's a long story.

Within two minutes I was negotiating the mean streets of Wichita. Traffic was virtually nonexistent. There were four inches of snow on the ground by then, and this got me to thinking about snow shovels. But I put that out of my mind. I had more important things to think about than the fact that Gavin had cleverly arranged for me to be the only son at home when Maw started looking for a strong back.

Maybe I had been wrong after all.

Maybe I should have destroyed Gavin earlier in the evening. Maybe I should have told Maw about the kitchen chair, the lollipops, etc.

Too late now.

But I still might be able to destroy him after we unwrap our presents on Christmas day, just before the Avalanche play the Flyers.

CHAPTER 16

"Where is he?" I said, as I entered the pub.

Duffy was stooped over a cooler behind the bar. He stood up and began wiping his hands with a damp rag. "He's gone."

"Gone where?"

"I don't know. I tried to keep him here until you showed up, Brendan, but he was out of control. I was afraid I might have to call the police."

"How long ago did he leave?"

"Five minutes. I'm sorry, Brendan. I did my best to keep him on the premises, but he was bound and determined to find work."

"At eleven o'clock at night?"

"Like I told you, he's drunk. I'm sorry to have gotten you involved in this, but he asked me to call you."

I nodded. "You did the right thing, Mister Duffy. He can't have gone far. I'll track him down."

"Just call me Duffy," he said.

"Call me Murph," I said. "That's what Sweeney calls me."

"I know. By the way, has Sweeney rescinded the eight-six yet?"

"No."

"You oughtn't to have kidnaped and killed that man, Murph."

"I *didn't*," I said. "The whole thing was just a ridiculous misunderstanding."

He gave me the fish-eye.

"Ask Sweeney yourself," I said, getting annoyed. After you've been directly involved in what appears on the surface to be a shocking daylight kidnap/murder, people tend to doubt every little thing you say.

"I'll ask Sweeney when he calls on New Year's Eve," Duffy said.

Was Duffy sticking it to me, or just being logical? But he knew that Sweeney would be calling from Denver to report my unruly behavior to Maw. I can't keep a secret from Maw, God, or bartenders. My life is like a *TV Guide*.

I left the saloon. It was easy enough to spot Jimmy Callahan's footprints on the snowy sidewalk. There were quite a few sets of prints because Duffy's was located right on Douglas Avenue, but Jimmy was the only person wearing size fourteen boots.

I followed them for half a block, then looked farther ahead. It appeared to me that Jimmy had approached the front doors of other business establishments along the block, but they were closed for the night. This is one of the drawbacks of being unemployed: it kills brain cells.

I hurried back to my car. Jimmy had only a five-minute lead on me, so I could have followed his prints on foot, but I never do anything standing up when I can do it sitting down. It's sort of a motto.

I hopped into the Buick and started the engine. A 1954 Buick Special is a behemoth. It's like an old-fashioned Checker Cab. A man named Stew who works in the cage at the Rocky Mountain Taxicab Company is the world's foremost expert on Checker Cabs, so if you have no interest in the entire history of the Checker Cab company, stay away from Denver.

I pulled onto Douglas Avenue and drove slowly along the curb peering at Jimmy's bootprints. They crossed over to the next block. My heart nearly stopped when I saw an all-nite cafe up ahead. The marquee was lit up saying, "Eats." I stomped on the accelerator, which had little effect because a Buick weighs about two tons and has a Dyna-Flow transmission, which is nothing at all like a standard transmission. I felt a slight surge of speed, then I had to brake gently. Given the nature of this mission, stomping on the gas was unnecessary, but it felt cool.

When the Buick rolled adjacent to the front door of the cafe, I saw with relief that Jimmy's prints came back out of the entryway and continued on down the block. The manager of the beanery apparently wasn't interviewing drunk job applicants.

I stomped on the gas again, but nothing much happened. The car just kept rolling right along. Buicks are a lot like women—they don't respond immediately to my fancy footwork, but they get me where I want to go. I cruised past a saloon and saw Jimmy's footprints enter and then leave the premises. Two doors farther down, I saw his prints approach the door to an army recruiting office that was closed. Fer the luvva Christ, the man had a monkey on his back. I had to stop him before he enlisted in the Marines. Marine recruiting offices are open all-nite—that's the word on the street anyway.

Suddenly I saw something that scared me. I was approaching a well-lit intersection not far from the central downtown district. There were a couple of movie theaters open for business, as well as a few restaurants and lounges, and standing on one corner was a Salvation Army Santa Claus. He had one of those tripod stands with a donation bucket hanging from a chain. Correction: there were two Santas, and they seemed to be fighting. One of them looked like Jimmy.

I pulled over to the curb and hopped out.

It was him all right. His beard was lying in the gutter. He was trying to wrestle the bell out of the other Santa's hand.

"Jimmy!" I shouted.

A crowd had gathered. Teenagers were making smart-aleck remarks. I muscled my way between the Santas, which was a mistake. How many times had I heard referees comment on the inadvisability of stepping between Muhammad Ali and _____ [fill in the blank]. I heard a ringing in my ears.

❖

Teenage girls were giggling. I woke up lying on the sidewalk.

"Break it up!" a voice shouted, and the next thing I knew two Wichita cops were dragging me erect by the armpits.

I won't belabor the obvious. Callahan and I were apprehended for the most heinous crime imaginable—assault and battery on a Salvation Army guy. But as upset as he was, the SA guy finally managed to make it clear to the policemen that Callahan had merely approached him and asked if he could ring the bell for five minutes. Then he told them that I had tried to break up the ensuing battle over the bell.

"Now why would you want to ring the man's bell?" one of the cops asked Jimmy suspiciously.

Jimmy bowed his head with shame and shrugged. "I was thinking ..." he began in a tiny voice, but the cop told him to speak up.

"I was *thinking* maybe *his* boss would see me and offer me a *job*," Callahan said.

The cop tipped his hat back on his forehead and put his fists on his hips. I could tell by his body language that he was baffled beyond belief. It was after eleven o'clock at night, the Christmas season was drawing to a close, and the deadline for generosity was approaching fast—after tomorrow night people would no longer have to avert their eyes as they scurried past Salvation Army tripods.

But I understood.

Callahan was like a writer willing to work for free on the off-chance that an editor would be so impressed with the quality of his prose that the editor would magically begin paying for what he previously had been getting for free. This is a form of mental illness for which there is no known cure.

"Excuse me, officer," I said, as he put away the cuffs. "I know this man. He's unemployed. Friends said he had been despondent lately." I looked around to see if any newspaper reporters were nearby. I was afraid I might get in trouble for using one of their clichés without a degree in journalism.

It took a few minutes to sort things out, but the SA Santa did not want to press charges, so the cops told me they would turn Jimmy over to me if I promised to see to it that he didn't look for any more work that night. "Your friend doesn't need a job, he needs a drink," the cop said.

I played it cool. I said I would drive Jimmy to the nearest bar right away. But after we got into my car, I told Jimmy he was going home.

"What's your address?" I said.

He lived in an apartment building a few blocks south of Kellogg Avenue, back in the direction of Duffy's. I reached out to drop my flag and start my meter, then shook my head with disgust and pride. Once an asphalt warrior, always an asphalt warrior.

By the time we pulled up in front of his apartment building, Jimmy's head was beginning to clear. "I gotta stop looking for work," he said.

"I hear you, man."

"But it's hard," he said. "Every morning when I wake up, the first thing I want to do is put on my shoes."

"Hey, I've been there," I said. "I was unemployed in Philadelphia for six months, and during the first week I woke up every morning and left my apartment."

"Where did you go?"

"That's just it. I didn't go anywhere. A couple times I walked around the block. It was like I was on a treadmill and couldn't get off."

"But you got off it, didn't you?"

"Yeah, but I did it the hard way."

"How's that?"

"Cold turkey. When I woke up in the morning I had to force myself to lay there and stare at the ceiling. I started having hallucinations. I heard foremen telling me to get my ass in gear. It was a living hell. But I stuck it out. By the end of the week, the voices had faded and I was sleeping till noon. The rest is history."

Jimmy was clutching both hands on his lap. "I don't know, Murph. I don't think I can go cold turkey. I mean ... it's easy right now to say I won't get up every morning and look for a job, but when the alarm goes off and I open my eyes, I just know I won't be able to fight the urge."

"First off, get rid of that damn alarm clock," I said. "If God intended you to wake up at sunrise, He would have given you a rooster."

Jimmy nodded, but it was the kind of nod that people make when they're sort of lying.

"Listen," I said. "If you can't go cold turkey, here's what you do. Taper off. Instead of looking for a job, buy a newspaper and read the want-ads. It's almost as good as applying for work, but not as risky. Nobody ever gets a job from the want-ads. But that way you can *pretend* to be looking for work. It's a mind game, I know, but self-delusion is your only hope. It works for me."

Jimmy gave me a wan smile. "I'll give it a try, Murph. Anyway, thanks for coming to get me. I won't bother you with my problems anymore."

"Hey, I make a living being bothered by people," I said. "I'm a professional taxi driver. You might want to give some thought to becoming a cabbie."

"I appreciate your advice," he said with a nod. "I guess I'll head in. Thanks for everything, Murph. Merry Christmas."

"Merry Christmas to you, Jimmy," I said. I handed him the remains of his beard. I waited as he got out and walked up to the door of his apartment building, then I reached for my meter again. I shook my head with exasperation. We all have our crosses to bear.

I drove back home thinking about Jimmy. A painful case that one, all right. I mean, why would a seemingly normal, intelligent person want a job? But that's the insidious nature of work. Personally I think society is to blame. At the age of five they send you off to kindergarten just to get you used to the idea of going somewhere every day. And since all you do in kindergarten is play with wooden blocks, you say to yourself, "Hey, this school stuff isn't half bad." But then they ship you off to grade school, and suddenly you're introduced to this thing called "homework." At first you think it's a joke.

Yeah.

Some joke.

I call it "The Twelve-Year Joke."

It's true that they teach you how to read and write and figure arithmetic, and there's nothing wrong with that—I often do those things—but by the fourth grade there's nothing left to learn. You know everything you need to survive as an adult, but do they let you stay home? Heavens no. They keep you rising at dawn for the next eight years. They keep you seated at a desk all day. And pretty soon you start thinking this is normal. And it is. That's the crying shame of it. It's perfectly normal. By the time you get your diploma, you don't know how to do anything else. It's *The Norm.* In other words, you have been programmed to get up and go somewhere for the rest of your life.

But here's the catch: at the age of sixty-five they tell you to stay home. Stay home?

How the hell do you do that?

Did they *teach* you how to stay home? Did they offer you classes in puttering? Did they instruct you in the finer points of uselessness? Hah! But at sixty-five they turn you loose in your bed and expect you to stay there.

The irony, of course, is that we are all born useless. Yet it takes us sixty-five years to get back to square one—unless you drive a cab. In most states a citizen can legally become useless at twenty-one.

Aah, why complain? It's all a racket. The only way to avoid it is to be born rich, or else win the lottery. That gives me a fifty-fifty chance. Best odds I'll ever get. They say that in Las Vegas you have a 2 percent chance of beating the house at Blackjack if you have a brain the size of Texas. I'll stick with scratch tickets.

I got home around twelve-thirty and pulled into the driveway. I eased the car into The Garage, *The Garage!* I shut off the engine. I liked driving that old Buick, and wished I could inherit it someday, but I knew my primogeniture brother was first in line to get the good stuff. A 1954 Buick Special in perfect running condition would be worth a lot of money in car-crazy California. I put it out of my mind. I do that with almost everything.

I slid the garage door closed and walked up to the back door of the house, then I stopped dead. I saw something that scared me. Leaning against the wall was a snow shovel. Strange. It hadn't been there earlier. Then I realized who had put it there. I was onto her. Maw was heavily into mind-control, too. I considered surreptitiously depositing the shovel in the Mulvehill trashcan, but it was only a passing thought. I couldn't put anything past my Maw except girly magazines, and I wasn't entirely certain about that.

CHAPTER 17

If X = oof, and Y = grunt, then 200(X+Y) = a shoveled sidewalk.

I got back in the house by nine a.m., dripping sweat in the middle of winter—my favorite thing next to whiskers on kittens. Maw had a fresh pot of hot chocolate percolating on the stove, but I was dying of heat prostration. Snow shoveling has a lot in common with hangovers. I drank two glasses of ice-cold water from the tap before I sat down at the kitchen table for a delicious cup of hot Nestle's Quick.

"What time are the relatives getting here?" I said.

"They'll be filtering in around eleven," Maw replied.

She was hurrying around the kitchen the way mothers traditionally do when they're cooking for a mob.

"Do you need any help?" I said.

Maw laughed like she always did. This had annoyed me when I was ten. At that age I firmly believed that, given the opportunity, I could be of immeasurable service to humanity. I did get the "immeasurable" part right.

Maw was still laughing when I arose from the table and sauntered into the living room. I was sauntering, it's true, but I have to admit it made me feel guilty to hear Maw rushing around banging cupboard doors open and closed, setting pots and pans on countertops, and sorting silverware. I can't stand to see people hurry.

Well, what the heck, it was Christmas Eve and the relatives would be arriving for the big afternoon meal and there was nothing I could to do to prevent it, although I gave it some thought as I channel-surfed for *Gilligan's Island*. No dice. It was Saturday morning and there were mostly cartoons on the channels I look at. Adult fare like *Gilligan's* apparently didn't come on until later in the ... suddenly I stopped surfing. I caught a glimpse of something familiar. I backed up the remote and squinted at the screen. Crimeny! It was the bane of my childhood, the Destroyer of Saturdays: *Weekend Gardener*. A moan welled up in my throat and I quickly punched the remote.

I didn't stop until I landed on *Bugs Bunny*. You have to understand—when I was ten years old, *Weekend Gardener* signaled the end of the morning roster of kid shows on Saturday. This was back in the days when we had only three channels to choose from. PBS was not a channel. Never was, never will be. So I would be sitting there in front of the TV happily eating Sugar Pops and watching *Ruff and Ready* or *Crusader Rabbit* and suddenly this violin music would leap from the speaker and an old man in bib overalls would say, "Today we'll be transplanting tulip bulbs." It always caught me off guard. I don't know who that man was, but he was no Mister Greenjeans. He forced me to do something that you might not believe: I voluntarily turned off the TV and ran out of the house. Need I say more?

But those days were gone. Cable had arrived to save the children. I envy today's kids. The fact that today's kids and I live on the same planet and in the same time-continuum should nullify the necessity for envy, but it doesn't.

The relatives began filtering in at eleven on the dot. My sisters came first, not surprisingly. Maw had forbidden them to show up before eleven to "help out." I understood my Maw's attitude perfectly. Maybe I do have a wavelength. Maw ruled the kitchen like

Sauron and wasn't interested in her female offspring's East Coast college-educated home-ec child-development theories about cabbage boiling.

Gavin showed up fifteen minutes later.

"You did a nice job on the sidewalk, kid," he said, as he sauntered past.

Then the uncles and aunts started arriving. I began flexing my fingers. I was in for a lot of handshaking. The women, aunts mostly, were carrying bowls of food: corn on the cob, sweet potatoes, fruit salad, the works. The men consisted of my mother's brothers and my father's brothers. Catholic. Numerous. Let's move on. There were other men but I didn't know who they were, whether friends of my uncles, husbands of my aunts, or vagabonds scoured from the highways and hedges. That's my favorite Biblical story, where the guy who has no friends invites hobos to his party. Been there.

Pretty soon the house was noisy. Kids were screaming and racing up and down the stairs. Girls dressed in snowsuits were crying because "the boys" had hit them in the faces with snowballs. The TV remote was taken over by the handshakers, and the sports channels were being surfed. You don't really need a description of the rest of the scene do you? Don't you have a family? Haven't you ever heard noise?

It abated at two in the afternoon when Maw announced, "Dinner is served!" I came out of the upstairs bathroom at that point and went downstairs. It turned out that my thirteen-year-old nephew Steven had been looking for me, possibly for the past two-and-a-half hours, but he didn't have any luck finding me because apparently nobody cared where I was.

"I have something to show you, Uncle Brendan."

"What?" I said suspiciously.

"See what I got for Christmas?" he said, holding up a couple of toy two-way radio transmitter/receivers.

I stared at them in disbelief. "Christmas isn't until tomorrow," I said. "How did you get your hands on these?"

"Mom lets us kids open one gift on Christmas Eve."

"What!" I almost screamed, but didn't.

"Really?" I said, but I was seething inside. Sally and her East Coast college-educated blah blah blah. Why would she let her children open a gift on the day before Christmas? Waiting until Christmas morning is what the holiday is all about: making kids suffer.

"Do they actually work?" I said.

"Yes, Uncle Brendan." Then he went into this complicated procedure of showing me the batteries and turning on the transmitters and explaining how they functioned, which I already knew because I'm a professional taxi driver. But I tried not to be smug about it.

We stood five feet away from each other and held a conversation.

"Breaker, breaker," I said.

"I see smokies," he replied.

We laughed. It never occurred to me how banal radios were until that moment. Unless tips are involved, what's the point?

"These are cool," I said to him.

Was I lying? I don't think so. When I was a kid, I would have sold my soul for a two-way radio. A couple tin cans and fifty feet of string were as high-tech as it got in those days. Then I almost did something that scared me. I started to tell Steven about the tin-can phones but abruptly stopped. I swear I heard my father's voice coming out of my throat. He was pontificating about the thrill of rolling barrel-hoops down a dirt road. It was like hearing Maw talk about the supremacy of radio over television. I coughed and cleared my throat and changed the subject.

"I use a two-way radio in my cab," I said.

"I know," he replied. "That's why I showed these to you. I thought you would be interested."

What the heck, he was just a kid. He would eventually learn that nobody is interested in anything.

"Let's grab a seat at the table," I said.

I was glad Steven was there. I asked him to sit on my left side at the "big" table. I could tell he felt proud to be included with the grownups. The rest of the kids were seated at the "little" table set up in the living room. The fact that I was using Steven as a human sandbag between myself and an uncle farther to my left did nothing to diminish the spirit of this joyous occasion.

"Brendan," Maw said. "Would you care to say grace?"

It was a rhetorical question. I sort of blacked out for a minute there, but when I came to everybody was saying "Amen," so I guess I got through it okay.

I'm not going to describe in detail the dinner and the lively conversations among the aunts, uncles, sisters, and evil brother. Just think of a Norman Rockwell painting with two turkeys on the table. If that doesn't work, read "The Dead" by James Joyce. It's a fine short story. Joyce didn't lose his way as a writer until he tackled novels. Been there.

Wellsir, things were going smoothly at my mother's house that afternoon, and then I got my bright idea.

It was related to the guilt I felt at having walked out of the kitchen at nine in the morning leaving my Maw to work hard. The fact that she didn't want my help did not alleviate my guilt. Nothing can alleviate Catholic guilt. It can only be shunted to the rear by newer guilt.

It all started after the family finished eating dinner and began drifting into the living room to watch TV, or to just sit and digest. The men dismantled the "little" table and the women began clearing the dishes and silverware. I went into the kitchen to get an American beer and saw the dishes stacked sky-high in the sink.

That was the precise moment when I got my bright idea. "You don't have to do the dishes, Maw," I said.

She was already pulling on her Playtex gloves in preparation for diving into the suds. She was alone in the kitchen right at that moment. The rest of the Murphy women were in the dining room gathering up the last of the dinner accoutrement, including the lace-curtain Irish hand towels that Maw brought out at Christmas in lieu of paper napkins. When it was just me and her at the table, I was given a paper towel. Anyway, I grabbed the rubber gloves.

"Just what do yeh think yer doing?" she said.

I took her by the elbow and escorted her out of the kitchen. "You and the rest of the ladies have done a fine job today and you deserve a rest," I said. "We men will do the dishes later. I want all the ladies to sit down and relax."

Everybody in the living room heard this. The aunts got blank looks on their faces, and the uncles smiled those wrinkle-faced, charming Irish smiles that you see whenever traditions are flaunted.

"Don't be ridiculous, Brendan," Maw said, and she made a move to step past me into the kitchen, but I blocked her path.

"I want you to sit down in front of the TV and take a load off, Maw."

"Stop acting like an infant," Maw said, as she feinted left and ducked right. But I was onto her. I backed up to the kitchen doorway and used my body as a sandbag.

"We men will be glad to take care of the dishes later," I pronounced, holding up an index finger.

"Brendan!" Maw sputtered. It was an actual sputter. "Let me by!"

"No Maw, you deserve a rest. And you know I can't digest food while people are working."

By now the aunts had started gathering around behind Maw like … well … did you ever see *The Birds*? I'm talking the scene where Tippi Hedren is sitting by the playground and doesn't see the crows behind her until hundreds are perched on the monkey bars.

My aunts were like that.

"We men will get around to doing the dishes later, right, men?" I said, raising my voice.

"That's right!" Uncle Patrick said. He was sipping a stout.

"Don't be ridiculous," Maw said. "Let's just do dishes right now and get them out of the way."

"Uncle Patrick, Uncle Michael, come and get your wives," I said, only I said it funny, ya know?

All the Murphy men rose from their chairs grinning and came into the dining room and took their wives by the shoulders and led them into the living room and made them sit down.

But the women got right back up. While this was happening, Maw said, "Let's just get the dishes done and get them out of the way." She tried to edge past me, but I kept blocking the doorway.

My mother's statement was taken up by the rest of the women. It became an ominous chant. "Let's get it done and get it out of the way." They massed in the center of the dining room and formed a flying wedge.

They came at me.

My uncles ran back in and started grabbing wives left and right, but the women wriggled loose and charged me again. Two of my uncles wormed their way through the melee and took up stances beside me so there were three bodies blocking the doorway.

"We'll do the dishes later!" I shouted.

"Nonsense!" Maw shrieked.

"Let's get it done and get it out of the way! Let's get it done and get it out of the way!"

One of my aunts made a break for the front door. Other women took off after her and I realized what they were doing. "Reinforcements!" I shouted, and two more uncles elbowed their way through the crowd and blocked the kitchen doorway.

I hit the back door just as Aunt Beth was pushing it open.

"Let's get it done and get it out of the way! Let's get it done and get it out of the way!"

"Uncle Patrick!" I barked. He charged into the kitchen and held the door while I shot the bolt.

I ran back toward the dining room and hollered at Steven, who was standing in the living room. "Toss me one of those radios!" He threw it over the heads of the women who were trying to breach my uncles. I grabbed it out of the air and pressed the button. "Steven, I want you to go outside and keep an eye on your aunts. Let me know what they're doing."

"Roger!"

I hurried to the back door and put my shoulder against it.

"Uncle Brendan!" Steven shouted over the radio.

"What!"

"Six ladies are making a pyramid by the window!"

I saw Aunt Polly's head rise above the sill. She was sliding the window open.

"Good Lord!" I choked. "Come on, Uncle Pat!" We ran to the window and forced it shut.

"Watch her fingers, watch her fingers," he said. He was a carpenter by trade.

But this turned out to be a classic diversionary tactic worthy of Rommel. While Patrick and I were busy with the window, the door to the basement burst open and aunts flooded into the kitchen. "Let's get it done and get it out of the way! Let's get it done and get it out of the way!"

I raised the transmitter to my lips. "We've got women in the wire! Women in the wire!"

Steven yelled something about the cellar door standing open, but it was too late.

Aunts grabbed sponges and hit the spigot. Our defenses collapsed.

Ladies poured in from the dining room. They threw us out.

Uncle Patrick and I slouched into the front room and sat down on the couch.

"I bet you went on sick-call a lot in the army, huh?" my evil brother Gavin said.

CHAPTER 18

At four-thirty p.m. on December 24th, I finally went Christmas shopping.

There are some things in life that you just have to do, and eating is one of them. Another is shopping. Eating and shopping converge at a nexus that I refer to as "The Big Grind," a phrase that actually encompasses more than mere food. Clothing falls into The Big Grind, which is why I shop for clothes only once a year, i.e., T-shirts, jeans, socks and one pair of Keds. I usually do this in the springtime when the earth (and me) is being reborn. I don't know what the connection is, but I think it has something to do with my English degree, specifically *Sir Gawain and the Green Knight*.

Christmas shopping is a grind that I experience once every twenty years. The Fourth of July, on the other hand, is never a grind. I always shop for my firecrackers in Wyoming, since the sovereign State of Colorado doesn't believe that children should be engaged in tomfoolery with explosive devices, but let's keep politics out of this.

Maw let me borrow the Buick again to do my shopping. The stores would close at six p.m. I know what you're thinking—the same thing Maw thought: Yeh put it off until the last minute, didn't yeh boy-o? Well, you're right, but there are two reasons for this. #1. I hate shopping. #2. I'm a man. Now that we've got that out of the way, let me add that I have learned how to do everything I hate in less time than it takes the average Woody Allen movie to run from FADE IN to ROLL CREDITS, i.e., ninety minutes.

I first started hating Christmas shopping when I was ten years old. Prior to that I had never done any Christmas shopping because I never had any money and my parents wouldn't give me any. But then, when I was ten, Maw decided to allow Gavin and myself to shop for presents. Her strategy was to lessen her own shopping burden.

Me ol' Dad never did any Christmas shopping. I don't know if that was pre-1960s sexism, or just the way things were, but one day Maw called Gavin and me into the kitchen and handed us six dollars apiece plus bus fare, and told us that we could go downtown and buy a present for each member of the family.

I have to be perfectly honest here: handing me six dollars at the age of ten was like the State of Colorado handing me a cherry bomb. On the ride downtown, I suggested to Gavin that we stop in at the penny arcade. This was a storefront arcade that we had been to many times, usually after going to the movies. We used the arcade to "cool down" after watching horror movies such as the *The Tingler* or *House on Haunted Hill,* as well as such forgotten classics as *The Wasp Woman, The H-Man,* and *The Horrors of the Black Museum* where (my apologies to the faint-of-heart) a man gets his eyes stabbed by nails inside spring-loaded binoculars. We needed a nightcap after those matinees, and the arcade was where we got it. Gavin always played the pinball machines. He had no use for the other devices, such as the target-shooting machines, the crane that theoretically picked up gold wristwatches and delivered them down a chute, or my bête noir, Skee-Ball.

For those of you who aren't familiar with this game, Skee-Ball is like a miniature bowling alley where you roll softball-sized wooden balls toward holes in a bull's-eye target and win coupons that can be redeemed for inexpensive plastic crap.

I later learned that Gavin had spent his own personal allowance money on the ten-cent pinball games. He was an altar boy and a Boy Scout on the cusp of Eaglehood. I, on the other hand, was me. I dug into the six dollars and played Skee-Ball at a nickel a game until I had the blind staggers. I had never done so much of anything in my life. It was like owning a Skee-Ball machine. I blew five of the six bucks. Gavin finally walked up to me and said, "Come on, Brendan, let's go do our Christmas shopping now."

It was only then that I realized I had one dollar left to spend on Maw, Dad, Gavin, Mary, Sally, and Shannon Lucy. To this day, I don't know what one dollar divided by six people is, and I don't want to know.

During our shopping spree Gavin bought normal things like toy teacups, cheap perfume, tie clasps, and so forth, and I bought things like plastic whistles. I tried to keep Gavin from seeing what I was buying, but he had eyes, he could see the tiny sack I was carting around. On the ride back on the bus he grabbed the sack to see what I had gotten him for Christmas. His present was a red comb that I had redeemed with my thousands of Skee-Ball coupons. After we got home, he "told."

That was one of the few times in my life that my Maw did not pretend I was Danny Mulvehill. She actually got mad at me. I would like to say that I learned my lesson that day, but let's move on.

I drove the Buick toward the central downtown district where I saw people just like me rushing in and out of buildings. This made me laugh because the similarity was only apparent. When I stopped at red lights I noted Salvation Army Santas still working the inter-sections, and this made me think of the painful case. I was torn. I wanted badly to convince Jimmy Callahan to give up his dream of

getting a job and simply go to work for one of the Wichita cab companies, preferably Yellow Cab. Call it name recognition, but there
was no Rocky Mountain Taxicab Company in Wichita, and Yellow
was like a reliable vintage wine. You could climb into a Yellow Cab in
Bangor, Maine, or Los Angeles, California, and you wouldn't know
the difference, except L.A. cabbies wear cool shades. I felt that if
I hooked Jimmy up with Yellow, I would be leaving him in good
hands when I left town.

But the problem was that this would take some effort, and I
am innately opposed to effort. Plus, I wasn't getting paid to help
him. Most of the people I had attempted to help over the years had
been cab fares, so I usually came out ahead financially in the end. Of
course profit wasn't my motive, but like a novelist who insists that
he has no interest whatsoever in money, I certainly would not turn
down a million dollars if Scribner's happened to offer me a goddamn
three-book deal!

Anyway, I was torn. I dealt with this by putting Jimmy out of
my mind. With luck I wouldn't remember him until I got back to
Denver, where I couldn't help him anyway.

I cruised around downtown until I spotted a large bookstore,
one of those national franchises that offer 40 percent discounts on
books. As an unpublished novelist, I was fully aware that those behemoth chain stores were driving the small independently owned
bookstores out of business all across the nation, but hey, I only had
an hour to shop.

I parked at the curb, put a quarter in the meter, and walked into
the store.

It took nine minutes—a record, but it was no Christmas miracle. I had twenty-seven shopping years of grind under my belt to
guide me. A little Dickens for Maw, a handful of coffee-table books

for my sisters, spy thrillers for the men, and a stack of kids' books for my nieces and nephews.

See ya next year.

I was back on the road before my quarter was fully digested by the parking meter.

But I was faced with a serious problem. Everybody in the family knew I had gone Christmas shopping, so if I returned after half an hour, they would know I hadn't put much thought into their presents. This was both true and untrue. I had long ago learned that books are the best presents you can buy for a person—except me. I like toys. But the point is, books last longer and aren't as easy to break, like almost everything else you can buy in today's free market. Call me an English major, but I happen to believe that books are more substantial than pet rocks, hula hoops, and most fruitcakes. But not everybody thinks like I do.

For one thing, I have learned that some people feel that books are "intrusive," in the sense that books put things into their heads that they don't want there. Some people call these things "ideas." Maybe they're right. Sometimes these ideas sprout into what are known as "thoughts," and you know my feelings about school, government, and big business—thoughts are the last things they want rattling around inside people's heads because thoughts inevitably lead to consumer protection, free speech, and hippies!

I seem to have gotten political here.

Anyway, it takes so little time to buy books that most people don't take them very seriously as gifts. By "people" I mean members of my family. Maybe they're right. I don't know what the time-factor has to do with it. Sure—it takes only nine minutes to buy a couple-dozen books, but if you add up all the years it took to write those presents, you've got a pretty feeble counter-argument.

Then I saw him.

He was standing on a street corner ringing a bell. You know who I mean: Jimmy Callahan. He was wearing a Santa Suit.

Fer the luvva Christ.

I drove around the block wondering how he had managed to get his hands on a job at this late hour. It kind of scared me. He was standing next to a Salvation Army tripod. For all I knew, he had done away with the real SA guy. The moment that a man becomes obsessed with the unbridled craving for work, anything can happen. I had to find out fast what he had done, and if possible, get him drunk.

I parked down the block, far enough away so he wouldn't notice me. As soon as I got out of the car I heard an ominous sound: "Clang-clang. Clang-clang." It sent chills down my spine. It reminded me of the surreal scene in *The Hunchback of Notre Dame,* where Charles Laughton is lying on his back shoving giant bells with his feet. But almost everything reminds me of that.

Just before I arrived at the spot where Jimmy was standing, I looked down at the snow-covered sidewalk. I was hoping I wouldn't see signs of a struggle—bloody snow, a furrowed path indicative of a body dragged into a nearby alley where a dumpster would conceal the results of his heinous crime until such time as he could make a daring escape.

"Howdy, Murph." I looked up.

Jimmy was smiling at me.

"Have you gone *mad!*" I shouted. The clanging stopped.

"I'm parked down the block," I said, with suppressed anxiety. "This is your only chance. Let's get out of here."

He hung his head with what I interpreted to be shame. "I'm sorry, Murph. I tried not to work, but I couldn't resist."

I calmed down.

"Where's the body?" I said.

"What body?"

"Don't get coy me with me. You know what body. The guy who's supposed to be working here."

He swallowed hard and began getting shifty-eyed. I knew the look. I patented it. I'm talking ©1958, baby.

He raised a thumb and pointed at a nearby coffee shop. "In there," he said.

I looked at the coffee shop. I saw a Santa sitting at the counter eating a donut.

"Oh no," I said. "Don't tell me. Say it isn't so. You aren't getting *paid,* are you."

It wasn't a question. It was a blanket condemnation.

He shook his head no.

What could I do with a guy like this? You can't *make* people stop working, they have to *want* to stop. He was like a writer who would stoop to anything to see his words in print.

"I sort of paid him," Jimmy said in a tiny voice.

"What?"

"I paid that man ten bucks to let me ring the bell for half an hour."

Oh my God.

Jimmy had hit rock-bottom. I'm talking vanity press.

I looked at the fat and sassy Santa sipping joe in the warmth of the coffee shop, then I looked at my wristwatch. It was ten minutes to six.

"Let me guess," I said. "You have ten minutes left on the clock."

He nodded.

I remembered how back in the days when I worked for Dyna-Plex

I had set my watch ahead ten minutes to trick myself into believing my life wasn't a living hell. It worked.

Ergo …

I raised my wristwatch, twisted the hands to six p.m., and held the watch up to his eyes.

"Time to call it a day, Jimmy."

He started to raise his own wrist, but I grabbed it. "We need to talk, Jimmy."

I gently eased the bell out of his hand.

I carried it to the coffee shop. I stepped inside and set the bell on the counter in front of the Santa. His eyes got as big as ping-pong balls.

Nuff said.

I walked outside, escorted Jimmy down the block, and stuffed him into the Buick. Then we went looking for a bar. Specifically a pub. I knew where I could find one fast. I used to sip soda there when I was a wee lad. I knew it so well that I could have driven there blind.

So to speak.

CHAPTER 19

Happy Hour was just coming to an end and Duffy was wiping down the bar. There were still a lot of people present though. The temporal end of all Happy Hours is more of an illusion than a reality, so it usually takes customers awhile to catch on to the fact that they have to stop being happy. Frankly, I think the bartenders want it that way.

Duffy took one look at the two of us and froze, except for his eyes. They were batting back and forth between us. For the first time in my cab-driving career, I could not read a pair of eyes. When you've driven a cab as long as I have, you see a lot of eyes in your rearview mirror, but they rarely bat. I'll admit I've seen a few flutter, mostly after picking up at The Lulu Room, but I couldn't tell if Duffy was shocked at seeing one of us in particular, or both. He quickly clarified things.

He stepped around the bar fast, took me aside and said quietly, "I'm sorry Murph, but you can't bring that laddie in here."

I was shocked. Had Jimmy been 86'd? "Why not, Duffy?"

"Because there's daycent people in here, and I don't want Jimmy creating a ruckus by applying for work again."

"You don't have to worry," I said. "Jimmy's just here to get drunk. He won't apply for a job, I promise."

Duffy gave me the fish-eye.

I was used to this. I knew how to handle it. I relaxed every muscle in my face until I looked mature. It's a trick I picked up in court.

"Your word of honor, Murph?"

"My word of honor, Duffy."

"As a cab driver?"

Whoa.

The Big One.

If I violated that oath, I would never be able to show my face in any saloon in America—and if The Word was spread among the cabbies of America, I would be *branded*. You wouldn't believe the complex grapevines I wrestle with as a taxi driver.

I swallowed hard. I don't think Duffy saw me swallow because I glanced down at my wristwatch at that precise moment so my chin would hide my Adam's apple. It's a trick I developed around parole officers.

"What'll it be then, eh?" Duffy said, heading back to the bar.

"Jimmy will have a shot and a beer," I said. "I'll have a cup of joe. I'm the designated driver."

Duffy went to work on the order while I herded Jimmy to an empty booth near the rear. We took off our coats and lay them on the seats and slid into the booth. Some of the customers began staring at us. I suggested that Jimmy remove his fake beard and pointy hat. I don't like people staring at me in bars unless I'm singing loudly.

After Duffy brought our drinks, I took a good look at the wretch seated across from me: Jimmy Callahan, former star center and all-state basketball champion of Blessed Virgin Catholic High School, reduced to working for a living. I couldn't believe it. When I was in high school, I thought all athletes went on to play for the pros. I mean, why else would anybody take verbal abuse from an ape five evenings a week?

During my freshman year in high school, I thought long and hard about whether or not I wanted to go out for intramural football and eventually land a job with the Kansas City Chiefs. Me ol' Dad was a Chiefs fanatic. He destroyed six different easy chairs during my childhood. He would get excited and howl and pound the arms of the chair—and that was just during half-time, so you can imagine what a commotion the game caused.

But the factor that dissuaded me from becoming a quarterback for the KC Chiefs was *Huckleberry Hound*. His cartoon show came on at five-thirty every evening during the middle of football practice. If it wasn't for Hanna/Barberra, I would probably have plastic knees right now.

Jimmy knocked back the shot, then chased it with a gulp of beer. At least I didn't have to teach him that. But how was I going to teach him to avoid work? My plan was to go beyond subtle hints and convince Jimmy to become a cab driver. However, I had learned over the years that most people view cab driving as a potentially dangerous occupation that doesn't pay well. I was going to play those facts down. I intended to emphasize the advantages, such as daily pay, a flexible schedule, and a virtually unenforceable code of personal hygiene. But in order to accomplish this, I had to incorporate techniques used by stage magicians, which primarily involved the art of D&D (distraction and deception). Pickpockets do this, too, but that's neither here nor there.

"Have you ever been married, Jimmy?" He shook his head no.

Hmmm. I had thought perhaps being burdened by the financial obligations that accompany marriage would explain his obsession with working. But since he had no wife, or children, or alimony payments, or child-support payments, I was at a complete loss. We both might as well have been ten years old.

"How about yourself?" he said, interrupting what I like to call my "train of thought."

"No, I never got married. I almost did though."

"What do you mean?"

"When I was at Kansas Agricultural University, I dated a girl named Mary Margaret Flaherty. I asked her to marry me but she turned me down. I proposed to her on the front porch of her parents' house one night."

"Oh yeah, I remember Mary," he said.

"Really?"

"Yeah," he said. "We had a couple of dates."

"Really?"

"Yeah."

"Really?"

"Yeah."

I couldn't stop saying really. I was like a scratched record. The thought of Mary Margaret dating anyone besides me had never entered my mind. I always assumed that after we broke up and I fled to Atlanta that she remained sitting on her front porch for all eternity. Not literally of course, but sort of. I mean, how could any woman possibly get on with her life after knowing me?

I sat there staring at Jimmy until he cleared his throat and said, "I sure could use another beer."

This brought me back to reality. Beer does that. I finally decided that a love affair that had ended almost a quarter-century ago had no relevance to the problem at hand. I was lying to myself of course, but I had to keep in mind the vow I had given to Duffy. I couldn't let myself get distracted by pathos. That road leads only to bathos.

"Have you ever had a big dream, Jimmy?" I said.

"Yes."

"I mean, have you ever reached for an unreachable star?"

"Yes."

"Let me put it this way. All my life ... well, ever since I grew up ... well, ever since high school, I've had one single overwhelming ambition that has guided my every waking moment."

"I know," he said.

"What do you mean, you know?"

"Mary Margaret told me."

"What did she tell you?"

"That you wanted to be a writer."

Goddamnit.

"Well, she was *wrong*," I said.

"That's what she told me. She said you dropped out of college to become a novelist. She told me on our fifth date."

Goddamnit!

"Listen," I said, "that writer stuff is just a way to get lots of money, but my *dream*, Jimmy, the dream that has never left me, the *big dream* that has guided me like a radar-controlled ICBM missile is to never again get up in the morning and go to a job."

Jimmy stared at me for a few moments. Then he picked up his glass, took a drink, and set it down. "That doesn't sound like a very realistic ambition."

I nodded. "It's not an ambition at all. That's the beauty of it. It's the complete absence of ambition."

He nodded slowly, as if he was beginning to understand. "I don't understand," he said. "Without ambition you would never do anything."

"On the contrary, you understand perfectly," I said. "Without ambition you would never do anything."

"That's what I said," he said.

We stared at each other in silence. It was as if Callahan and I were locked in a battle of the intellects so abstract that no mere mortal could have followed the subtle threads of logic that lifted us into a realm of consciousness incomprehensible even to Mister Spock.

"But how would you get money?" Jimmy said.

I coughed and cleared my throat. "You're missing the big picture," I said. "Step one is to divest yourself of all ambition. After you have succeeded in doing that, then—and only then—can you take step two, which is to figure out a way to get money."

"It seems like you should get the money first," Jimmy said. "Then you could go ahead and stop having ambition."

I took a deep breath and sighed. I hated talking to amateurs. They did everything exactly backwards.

"Listen," I said. "Suppose you got a lot of money first, okay? The ambition that got you the money would remain inside you because you hadn't done anything to get rid of it, right? Follow me?"

"Yes."

"So even though you've got money, the unexpurgated ambition would cause you to keep on *doing* things. But why would you do things if you had lots of money?"

"I wouldn't," he said. "That's why I think you should get the money first."

"But you *would* do things, don't you see? First you have to get rid of the ambition, otherwise you'll go on doing things to make even *more* money!"

"That's what I said," Jimmy said. "Then you could stop having ambition."

"But you *wouldn't* stop having ambition!" I yelled. "Don't you see? The ambition would still be *inside* you. You would be like a petri dish full of *salmonella.* You have to purge the ambition *first,* and then you can ..."

"I'm going to have to ask you to leave the premises, Murph."
I looked up.

Duffy was standing by the booth frowning. I got rattled.

"I'm sorry, Duffy, I swear Jimmy isn't applying for a job."

"It's not that, Murph. Jimmy is welcome to stay. It's you. Your line of faulty reasoning is upsetting my customers. I've been getting complaints."

"Faulty?" I said.

"Yeah," came a muffled voice. "You're a sophist."

I looked around to see who had said it. People were glaring at me. The smell of blood was in the air.

I curled my fists and stood up from the booth. "Look folks, I don't want any trouble, but it stands to reason that if a man wants to stay in bed all day, he can't have any ambition."

"Specious postulate," someone muttered.

I swung around to find the bastard, but Duffy touched me on the shoulder. "Please, Murph, don't make me call Sweeney."

That brought me back to reality. I looked at his face. He meant business. The phone was five feet away. I uncurled my fists and bowed my head.

"Please go, Murph," Duffy said. "You're not eighty-sixed. You can come back after you have revised your basic premise."

I felt desperate. I hadn't even touched on the subject of cab driving, which was what I had been leading up to. Fer the luvva Christ, the moment we sat down I should have just told Jimmy to apply for work at Yellow Cab.

I nodded and picked up my coat. I looked at Jimmy.

"Are you coming with me?"

He shook his head no. "I think I'll stick around for a few more beers."

I swallowed hard. I elbowed my way through the crowd and stepped outside of the bar. I heard mocking laughter at my back. Someone dropped a nickel in the jukebox and Elvis started singing "Wellll, it's Christmastime pretty baby ..."

I flipped my collar up, jammed my fists into my coat pockets, and walked to my car. I got in, started the engine, and turned on the windshield wipers. The presents I had bought for my relatives were resting in a paper sack on the front seat. I couldn't stand the sight of them. The presents I mean. I picked up the sack and set it in the backseat, then I turned and stared out the front window.

I was depressed. I had blown the opportunity to give a friend the best Christmas present ever: the gift of cab driving. That's even better than books because books end after a few hundred pages, but cab driving goes on forever.

Well, that was that. I was through trying to help people out. I decided it was time to take The Final Vow, the vow that I would stick with for the rest for my life. Never again would I ever get involved in the personal life of a friend, a taxi fare, or an unconscious guy sitting next to me on a bus. And since this was Christmas Eve, which is as close to Christmas as you can get without actually being there, I knew I would keep The Final Vow.

I put the car in gear, pulled onto Douglas, and headed home. When I got there, I saw a lot of cars parked out front, and this took my mind off my failure. Why were my relatives still at the house? This was a question I had asked myself hundreds of times when I was a kid.

Then I asked myself how I was going to sneak the presents into the house.

Under my shirt?

Disgusted, I pulled into the driveway, glided slowly into the garage and parked. It took me a moment to transfer the sack of books from the backseat to the trunk, where I figured they would be safely hidden until everybody was gone. Then I closed up the garage, walked to the back door, and entered through the kitchen.

"He's here!" someone shouted.

I froze.

My sister Sally walked into the kitchen with a gleeful smile. "You got back just barely in time, Brendan," she said, in a voice rampant with jubilation. "Guess what?"

"What?" I said disinterestedly.

"I talked the whole family into going Christmas caroling!"

CHAPTER 20

"It's only a movie … it's only a movie …" I mumbled as Gavin's rental car wended its way down the block.

We got out in front of the Weinstein's house. There were four cars chauffeuring all my sisters and their husbands and kids and me and Maw and my evil brother Gavin, who had stopped me from accomplishing two things during the brief flurry of loading the cars for the journey through Jayhawker hell. To wit: when I suggested that I drive Maw's Buick by myself in order to make room for others in his rental, he nixed it by making loud and exclamatory statements having to do with the possibility of me getting lost on the road and not being able to participate in the caroling from start to finish. My sisters took up the cause and I was relegated to riding in his backseat.

Gavin could read me like an X-ray.

But the other, and far more serious intervention on his part, was stopping me from making a run into the house to grab the nearest pint of anything. "No time, kid, no time! Let's hit the road!" and he stuffed me into the rear of his car.

I remember kids. Kids wrapped in wool. Little squirmy wool-wrapped noisemakers. Gavin was having a ball. I couldn't help but ponder the irony of the fact that if I hadn't gotten so pedantic back at Duffy's I wouldn't be in a backseat, I would be in a booth congratulating Jimmy Callahan for having the courage to drive a taxi instead of getting a job, and the wisdom to know the difference.

The Weinsteins apparently weren't home.

We piled into the cars and drove around to the other side of the block and piled out to sing carols in front of the home of one of Sally's friends from grade school.

"Joy to the world!!!..." I screamed at the top of my lungs.

The same thing happened at each of the thousands of houses we stopped at that night. We would start singing, a porch light would come on, and a minimum of two adults would open the front door and stand there smiling with a kind of ... I don't know ... wistful expression or something, while we knocked out three ballads before piling back into the cars. At a few of the houses the people asked if we would like to come inside for eggnog.

Eggnog.

I knew what was in eggnog, and so did my evil brother Gavin. I was the first to holler "Sure!" followed by Gavin hollering "No time! No time!" He had taken charge of this caravan like Josey Wales, except he liked it.

At one point I found myself sitting in the backseat with Steven, who looked about as somber as I felt. Or do I mean "sober"? His brothers, sisters, mother, and father were in a different car.

"Having fun?" I said.

I almost said, "Are we having fun yet?" but I try not to exude bitter sarcasm around kids. Kids don't always grasp sarcasm, and often take a question from an adult literally and try to give a correct answer to that which is not so much a question as a cry for help.

He shrugged.

I liked that.

We pulled up in front of a suburban house. This gave me hope. If we were "doing" the suburbs it meant we were running out of Wichita. Even though the possibility existed, I doubted we would be heading into the wilderness to carol at farmhouses. I had a passing acquaintance with farmhouses. I once went pheasant hunting with me ol' Dad when I was twelve. He was toting a twelve-gauge shotgun and I was toting a sixteen-gauge shotgun. I refer to this as "The Pheasant Hunting Incident." I will never tell you that story.

I began hoping that someone else would suggest it was time to go home. I knew it would be a waste of time for me to say it. The only pleasure I took in not suggesting that we bring this to an end was knowing that Gavin would not be able to articulate whatever sarcastic grenade he was itching to lob in my direction. Every time I looked at his eyes in the rearview mirror he was looking back at me, waiting for me to complain. But I merely smiled at him. It was another battle of the intellects. I average three a month in Denver, but I always have access to a getaway vehicle. I tell ya, not being able to drive a car that Christmas Eve made me feel helpless. It made me feel like a poor person. I don't know how poor people ever win arguments.

And then it happened. It was like that scene in *Cool Hand Luke* when George Kennedy suddenly stopped shoveling sand onto the hot tar and looked around with amazement and said, "We've run out of road!" My favorite film-fact about George Kennedy is that in 1954 he was a technical adviser on *Sergeant Bilko*.

"That's all she wrote!" Gavin hollered. We had run out of people to annoy.

I glanced at my wristwatch and saw that the entire incident had taken ninety minutes, the same as a Woody Allen movie, even though it felt like David Lean.

The caravan started back toward home. I relaxed in the backseat and closed my eyes, and the sensation of well-being was like the time I got on a bus after receiving my army discharge. "Get thee behind me, whatever you are," that's my motto.

When we arrived at the house, everybody came inside. Maw had hot cocoa simmering in a crockpot. The adults sat down to wait for cups to be filled, and the kids picked up running around screaming where they had left off. I can't say for a fact, but I do not remember running around screaming when I was a kid, although it is not beyond the realm of possibility. But it doesn't make sense to me because I spent most of my childhood sneaking around, and screaming doesn't fit into the paradigm.

It would be another fifteen minutes before everyone warmed up from the singing in the snow, so I decided to step out onto the front porch and smoke a cigar.

Maw doesn't let me smoke cigars in the house, unless she's having one, too. But she smokes only one cigar a year. She has her annual stogie on Christmas night. It's a tradition that started before I was born, just after World War II ended. Maw was a riveter in the Boeing Airplane plant outside Wichita during the war. That was back in the dark days when the women of America had to perform the work of the men who were fighting overseas, such as operating the black market. In later years, Maw and Pop used to light up on Christmas night while we kids fled to our bedrooms. Cigar smoke made us nauseous. Maw prefers Dutch Masters, but I'll smoke anything. Try me.

I stepped out to the porch and lit up a Swisher Sweets. The night sky was clearing. The stars were twinkling. It was like one of those beautiful, pristine, archetypal Christmas tableaus you see on gas station calendars. Then the front door opened and my nephew Steven came outside.

"Hi Steven," I said. I would have preferred to make a sarcastic quip having to do with his escaping from the noise, but as I said, kids don't always get jokes, and at the same time they are always prepared to cut and run at the first sign of condescension. I know the drill. I have uncles, too.

"Hello, Uncle Brendan."

"What's up?" I said.

"I want to talk to you about something."

I almost cut and ran. I never want anybody to talk to me about anything. But I couldn't just take off running down the street and leave a child standing alone on a porch in the middle of winter.

Or could I?

"What do you want to talk to me about?" I said.

"Grandmother told me that you were always the one with the sense of humor."

"*Who* said that?"

"Your mother."

"Oh … Maw. Right. She does say that. I guess I've always thought of myself as the male Phyllis Diller, except Phyllis already has that title."

It went right over Steven's head, thank God.

"So I was wondering if you would do me a favor, Uncle Brendan."

"What favor?"

"I would like you to listen to some jokes I wrote."

"Jokes?" I said. Whenever I'm driving my cab in Denver I often find myself saying, "Poems?" Not very often though. Poets usually take busses to wherever poets go.

"Okay," I said. "But why did you write some jokes?"

"Because I want to be a stand-up comic when I grow up." Yikes!

Advice started popping up like red flags. But I put a lid on it. Steven was young. He would doubtless be discouraged from following through on such an unlikely vocation long before he graduated from college. I had to remind myself that I was not in charge of the whole world, just Denver.

"All right," I said. "Hit me."

"What did one cyclops say to the other cyclops?"

"I give up."

"I'm so tired I can barely keep my eye open."

I chuckled even though I knew it would only encourage him—the worst thing you can do to a stand-up comic.

"Here's another one," he said. "Do you know why I think women are dope addicts?"

"Why?"

"Because they marry dopes."

I tried to tone down my chuckles, but didn't succeed. Then I told him that it might be best if he didn't tell that joke to his mother, or to any woman ever.

"So you write your own material, huh?" I said.

"Yes, Uncle Brendan."

"It's good pretty good stuff, but my advice would be to stick with the linguistic persiflage and leave the relationship jokes to Rodney Dangerfield."

"What does 'persiflage' mean, Uncle Brendan?"

"Go look it up in the dictionary, laddie."

"Okay."

He turned and walked back into the house. I was thunderstruck. I had never met an obedient child in my life. How did my sister do that to him? But I was glad he was acquiescent and had walked away. It saved him from getting more advice. When I'm driving my taxi you can't stop me from giving advice, but what kid wants advice? Steven just wanted laughs, I could tell. He was like a poet. He had embraced an unrealistic ambition. Who knows, he might even become an unpublished novelist someday. A lot of artists start out as failed poets, then move on to being failed short-story writers before they finally break through to the big time and become failed novelists. If they're like me, they branch out to become failed screenwriters. A few take the high road and become failed playwrights, but most just stick with being failed novelists because the potential to not make lots of money is greater.

I was finishing up my cigar when the front door opened and family members began trooping out, which may seem like a coincidence but it wasn't. Experienced cigars smokers know what I'm talking about.

I stubbed out the butt on the heel of my tennis shoe and began smiling and waving as the folks made their way down the steps and out to their respective cars. Seeing my relatives go away filled me with a special feeling of Yuletide joy. But then my sister Sally came out the door, stopped next to me, and said, "Brendan, there's something important I need to talk to you about."

It was like the scene in that movie where the roof caves in on what's-his-name, that actor—you know the movie I'm talking about.

"What is it, Sally?" I said in a strangled voice.

"I didn't want to talk about this until everyone was in their cars," she said in a muted tone of voice.

You have to understand—my sister Sally has always acted as if everything she says is imbued with deep significance. It runs in the family.

"What is it, Sally?" I said again.

"I have something to ask of you," she said.

"What is it, Sally?"

Getting to the point does not run in our family.

"I bought Steven a bicycle for Christmas, but it isn't assembled yet, and I was just *wondering* ..."

At this point her voice became high-pitched. I call it the "favor-asking" pitch. You may have experienced this yourself. I don't know why people raise their voices to above high C when they say, "*wondering*," but Sally's voice nearly shattered the porch light.

"... if you would assemble it for me."

"Where is it?" I said.

"It's hidden in the basement," she said, then she went into this business about how it would be impossible to assemble Steven's bicycle at the hotel blah blah blah, but I already had tuned her out. I don't know why people think long-winded explanations alleviate pain.

"... and Arnie is all thumbs," she finished, rolling her eyes.

"Who?" I said.

"My husband."

"Oh," I said. "Yeah, I'll do it."

If I remembered correctly, it was Archimedes who said, "Give me enough liquor, and I'll move the earth."

But after giving it some serious thought, I decided not to drink alcohol while I built the bike. I remembered one time in college when I got drunk, picked up an electric shaver, and decided to give myself a haircut. For the remainder of the semester I was known around the campus as "the cat in the hat."

I sat on the floor by the Christmas tree and sipped soda and pretended I was the Professor. You know what professor I'm talking about—the egghead created by Sherwood Schwartz, the protean genius whose sole function was to ensure that the television audience would find the survival of the castaways plausible. It apparently worked because the only thing I ever found implausible about *Gilligan's Island* was that it lasted three seasons.

CHAPTER 21

M aw went to midnight Mass on Christmas Eve. For you non-Catholics out there, midnight Mass starts at twelve midnight. It goes until about one o'clock in the morning depending on whether it's a standard Mass or the longer Latin Mass for the old pros, like my Maw.

My other siblings would be going to Mass in the morning, but Shannon Lucy and Maw had been going to midnight Mass ever since I was a wee lad. Shannon Lucy was the sister who had always talked about becoming a sister when she grew up. Catholic girls do that in the way Catholic boys talk about becoming priests. The altar boys I mean … not me.

I had already decided that if Maw asked me if I wanted to go to church, I would tell her the truth and confess that I didn't go to church anymore. I kept waiting for her to say something as she got fixed up to go, but she never said a word. When Shannon Lucy arrived in her rental, she didn't say anything either. Neither of them brought up the subject of my going with them. Their clever plan worked. I finally threw on my coat and went to Mass with Maw and Shannon Lucy.

It was a Latin Mass for the old pros.

It took me back to the days before Vatican II, the same year I started avoiding altar-boy practice. Monsignor O'Leary burned incense that night. If you're a non-Catholic and you've never smelled High Mass incense, brother, you don't know what you're missing.

I'm not even going to try to describe the deep, rich, sweet, rugged, earthy odor of aromatic smoke wafting from the polished silver censer, except to say that it makes you feel like your soul has been rinsed and repeated.

The next morning, a few close relatives arrived early at the house to celebrate Christmas: sisters, husbands, children. The extended uncles and aunts wouldn't be arriving until afternoon. But because I hadn't drank anything the night before, I was able to get out of bed as soon as Maw pounded on my bedroom door. "One hour!"

She didn't have to explain. She had explained it the night before while I was assembling the bicycle. She was watching one of the many versions of *A Christmas Carol* on TV. It was either the 1938 version with Reginald Owen or the 1966 Mister Magoo. I didn't pay any attention. I was too busy reading "instructions," as technical writers refer to the things they type.

While working on the bike, I started wondering about technical writers. Do they aspire to become Ernest Hemingway in their youths but then get sidetracked into instruction manuals? Or do they spend their early years leafing through refrigerator-repair manuals and dreaming their own version of The Big Dream? I envisioned a teenaged boy seated alone in his bedroom hunched over a Smith Corona and typing up a detailed assembly of a model car, and then wondering if he should submit it to a toy company on spec.

Do unpublished technical writers stand in drugstores reading labels on medicine bottles and dreaming about writing lists of active ingredients?

Then I wondered if the world of technical writing had its own literary demigods in the way that, for instance, the world of science fiction has authors like Robert Heinlein, "The Dean of Space-age Fiction." I envisioned two unpublished technical writers in their early twenties standing on a street corner and watching with awe as a nonde-script fellow in a suit walked by. "My god—look! That's Earl Beckman. He wrote the first Maytag dryer manual. I thought he was dead!"

I experienced my own brush with technical writing when I wrote brochures for Dyna-Plex. Fortunately none of the brochures involved telling people how to do anything. As best as I can recall, the brochures touched on reinventing wheels and thinking outside boxes. I never did learn what sorts of goods or services Dyna-Plex provided for its customers. If I ever have absolutely nothing to do and no reason to go on living, maybe I'll call the receptionist and ask her what they do there.

As a cab driver I give people advice all the time, but none of the advice comes from years of research, study, or experimentation. It is gleaned from the top of my head over a period of five seconds. I would never dream of writing detailed instructions for a crucial mechanical operation such as the installation of automobile brake drums.

I promise.

After I assembled the bicycle, I cleared a path in the living room and gave the bicycle a test run, making extra sure the brakes worked. The coup de grace was a red ribbon that Maw tied to the handlebars in lieu of making me wrap the bicycle—we had both seen *The Seven-Year Itch* often enough to know that some things just cannot be wrapped. We "hid" the bike in the kitchen. After that I wrapped my books. Maw was so engrossed in the TV show that she didn't notice the slim volume I had purchased for her. I crossed my fingers and hoped she would enjoy reading *A Christmas Carol.*

❖

My designated job on Christmas morning was to wait for an oppor-tune moment, then wheel the bicycle into the living room and watch as Steven's eyes lit up. I won't keep you in suspense. His did.

I was just finishing a breakfast of bacon and eggs fixed for free by my Maw when the doorbell rang. The Murphy clan had arrived. Gavin didn't seem too happy, so I looked forward to casually asking if he had run into any of the relatives in the hallways of the downtown Holiday, or even better, if any of the husbands had knocked on his door at midnight and asked if he wanted to run down to the lounge and catch The Bio Rhythms. I had not yet slept a single night in my room at the Holiday, and so far it was the best money I ever spent.

One of the husbands brought his home video outfit to capture forever these precious memories on tape. Me ol' Dad had used an eight-millimeter home movie camera, and I gotta tell ya, video is much better than film because you can use natural lighting. Most of our celluloid home movies consist of either total blackness or else closeups of faces squinting against the blinding glare of 500-watt bulbs. Me ol' Dad was no Cecil B. DeMille. He wasn't even Ed Wood. He was me ol' Dad.

The husband, whichever one he was, danced around the room with his video camera, setting up shots as each kid unwrapped his or her present. One present at a time had become the "new way" of doing things. When I was a kid we all tore into the presents like locusts, i.e., simultaneously. Christmas was over in two minutes. But because my sisters were now "modern" or something, they made each kid unwrap one present at a time in ascending order, meaning the youngest first. I knew it would take forever to get to me. But that wasn't the worst of it. Sally kept barking, "Don't tear the paper! Don't tear the paper! Save it for next year!"

Each kid had to carefully unpeel the tape and delicately unfold the wrapping paper and gently slip it off the box and hand it to Sally, who was lugging around a cardboard box for storage. She also yelled, "Save the bow!" if an especially pretty bow was removed from a package. The unwrapping of the presents went so slowly that the kids looked like WWII British demolition experts.

Then it was my turn. Even though my sisters were younger than me, they didn't open their presents ahead of me. I didn't know if this was because the ascending order officially became invalid after the age of thirteen, or if there was some other system at work that I failed to comprehend, but everybody started saying, "Open your present, Brendan!"

I figured there was still another hour to go before I went onstage, so it came as a surprise. I wasn't as psychologically prepared to be the center of attention as I usually am.

"Which one is it?" I said, shuffling toward the tree while everyone grinned at me. Fingers started pointing. Not at me but at a large box that had been shoved behind the tree at some point during the festivities. I hadn't even noticed it. Then it occurred to me that they had put it there while I was hiding in the kitchen getting ready to bring out Steven's bicycle. I grew wary. When you've been a Murphy as long as I have, you become hypersensitive to conspiracy. My family was "up to something." My imagination started to run amok. For one insane moment I thought I was going to find a job inside that box.

"All right, what's this?" I said in a voice imbued with mock disgust as if I was tired of all the nonsense and hadn't even wanted to be there in the first place. I'm pretty sure I fooled them.

I reached behind the tree and dragged the box out. It was heavy. It felt like a job on a loading dock.

"Don't tear the …!" Sally shrieked as I ripped the paper away from the box. "Oh *Brendan,*" she said mournfully. I had spent my entire childhood listening to people say, "Oh *Brendan.*"

The wrapping paper was ruined. A bit of tape might have put it in good enough shape to reuse next year, but I squelched that possibility by wadding it up and tossing it over my shoulder. All the kids laughed. I was setting a bad example. That's what uncles are for.

"What's this?" I said in a thin and querulous voice, indicating that I was asking a real question. I rarely do that.

I peered at the graphic artwork on the side of the box. It looked like a photograph of a TV set.

Nobody said anything.

I looked at the words below the photo. "Personal Computer," it said.

"Read the card!" Sally shouted. Our resident puppet-master liked to tell people what to do just before they did it.

The card was lying on the floor where it had fallen during my ripping spree. I picked it up and read the handwriting.

"Merry Christmas, Proust." It was signed "Gavin."

I looked around at Gavin, who was seated on an overstuffed chair. He was chewing a toothpick and smiling at me. Suddenly all I could think about was the flimsy spy thriller I had bought for him: *Kremlin Bloodbath*.

"Cool!" Steven shouted. He was sitting on his parked bike. He climbed off and came over to the box and knelt down beside it. "Wow, a RamBlaster 4000. This is state of the art, Uncle Brendan."

Due to the fact that I had been raised in the Murphy clan, I started to revert to a mode that I call the "Ritual of Refusal," a formal ceremony consisting of a number of vocal incantations that include such phrases as "Oh I can't accept this," and "This must have cost a fortune" ... as well as the ever-popular "Take it back." But I squelched it. I had been trying to wean myself from phony rituals ever since high school graduation.

"Thanks, Gavin," I said. I didn't know what else to say. Maybe it hadn't been such a good idea after all for me to turn my back on the verbal customs and traditions of polite social interaction shortly after being born.

Gavin removed the toothpick from between his teeth. "You're welcome, kid," he said, and put the toothpick back.

"Do you want me to help you set it up, Uncle Brendan?" Steven said.

I looked down at him. His eyes were as big as ping-pong balls. "Do you know how to set up computers?" I said.

"Sure! I got the RamBlaster 3000 for my birthday last year. It's almost the same, only this is better."

"I'm certain that your Uncle Brendan doesn't want to set that thing up until he gets back to Denver," Sally said, grabbing wads of wrapping paper off the floor and jamming them into the box. She seemed miffed. I wasn't surprised. I've never met a woman yet I haven't miffed.

"All right, Steven, you can help me," I said. "We'll haul it up to my room and put it on the desk where I used to pretend to do my homework."

"Okay!"

"Do we have time for that?" Sally said, frowning deeply and touching her lower lip with a fingertip. She was going into what I call the "Sally Emergency Mode." Any time Sally doesn't want somebody to do something, she pretends to fret about imaginary deadlines. All of a sudden I wished I hadn't ripped up the wrapping paper. I didn't want to ruin everybody's Christmas by getting Sally going.

"We'll just carry the computer upstairs and take a quick look at it," I said.

"Well, all right, I suppose, but we still have to finish opening presents, and then we're having cold-cuts ..." Sally muttered, gathering up the trash and itemizing her long-range agenda while Steven and I hauled the box upstairs.

I don't know if you know anything about computers, or teenage boys, but apparently no nerd has ever "looked" at a disassembled computer in his life. Steven had the machine up and running in five minutes.

After the monitor lit up, he told me that the peripherals were hidden in Gavin's bedroom. I started to panic. What the hell were *peripherals?* Strangers? Rules? Job applications? Turns out they were equipment, like disks and cables and a printer and all this other jazz that must have cost a fortune. Gavin hadn't wrapped them, he had just wrapped the big box. By now I was certain that Gavin had un-wrapped his pitiful little spy thriller and was on the phone asking Bill Gates to send a couple of goons over to repossess my computer.

Steven was showing me how to print when Gavin strolled in. He stood behind us and watched in silence for a while, then said, "Is he laarning anything, Stevie me boy?" Steven shrugged.

"Stevie was my freelance consultant on this," Gavin said. "After I talked to Tommy Malloy's sister, I decided to return the typewriter ribbons and buy you this instead."

"What's Tommy Malloy's sister got to do with it?" I said, turning around and looking up at Gavin.

"She told me that Tommy had made no progress writing his suspense novels until he bought a personal computer."

I knew where he was headed with that canard. I was the only writer left at Rocky Cab who still used a manual typewriter to pro-duce failed novels.

"Are you trying to tell me that a computer will make me a better writer?" I said, my voice imbued with surliness.

"I don't know anything about computers, and I don't know

anything about the writing of literature," Gavin said. "I only know that Tommy Malloy got a three-book deal from Scribner's after he bought his computer."

I smirked. "An obvious case of the generic fallacy," I said. "Just because the electricity goes out at the precise moment that you sneeze doesn't mean …"

"And there's talk of a motion-picture deal," Gavin said.

Urk.

The air in the room grew thin. I couldn't breathe. I swallowed a few gulps of oxygen and said, "Hollywood?"

Gavin nodded. He was smiling one of those thin-lipped smiles that mothers display when they know they've got their sons by the short hairs.

"This is called a 'spell-checker,'" Steven said, pointing at something on the screen.

I turned and looked at the computer. I worked my jaw a couple of times, then softly said, "What does it do?"

"It checks your manuscript for misspelled words and then it corrects them."

The room started to spin.

"And this thing here automatically counts the words in your manuscript," he said.

"Huh?"

"It's called a 'word-count.'"

Good lord. I remembered the time I had tried to manually count all the words in a horror novel I had written called Draculina. It took me three days, and at the last second I lost count. It was horrifying.

"Anyway," Gavin said, "Sally sent me up here to corral the two of you. Brunch has commenced."

I was hungry, but strangely I didn't want to leave the room. I didn't want to leave this miracle machine. I could feel myself drawn to it in the way that Bertie Wooster is drawn to Jeeves. I had never known that a PC performed all of these functions for its master. I always thought a word processor was merely a pretentious typewriter for yuppies. I didn't know it actually did stuff.

"Thanks for setting this up for me, Steven," I said. "We'd better go eat."

"Okay, but first let me just show you this one other thing, all right?"

"All right."

"This is a modem," he said.

"What does it do?"

"It lets you talk to everybody in the whole wide world."

"Why would I want to do that?" I said.

He shrugged.

I liked that.

We went downstairs. It was time to eat and I didn't want to hold up brunch, because this was America, and Americans are forbidden to feel hungry for more than ten seconds.

CHAPTER 22

Call it a Christmas miracle, but I decided not to destroy my brother that day.

I also stopped referring to him as "evil" both in my mind and in public. I'll admit it. I was embarrassed that Gavin had given me a RamBlaster 4000 instead of the usual carton of typewriter ribbons. Up until this particular Christmas day, I had always thought that Gavin was "sticking it to me" when my annual box of black ribbons showed up at my crow's nest in Denver. I always thought he was sending me a box of symbolism. I had never written him thank-you notes for the ribbons he had sent me over the years due to my misinterpretation of his gestures of kindness—that, and the fact that I'm a lazy bastard. My plan all along had been to use his sarcastic ribbons to write a best-selling novel and then mail the book to him with a devastatingly condescending note inscribed on the fly-leaf. Thank God I never sold anything.

But this gave me an idea for a novel called *Riff*. It would be the story of two brothers whose relationship was destroyed by a misinterpretation of the facts. I decided against it though. Frankly, I dislike autobiographical fiction. I prefer imaginary tales involving flights of pure fantasy, such as *A Farewell to Arms*. Face it—Ernest Hemingway was just a truck driver in the Italian army.

After brunch Steven and I went back upstairs. He showed me how I should go about assembling the computer after I got back to Denver. I hadn't paid such close attention to instructions since the day my taxi mentor, Big Al, showed me how to fill out credit-card receipts. Prior to that, I had never read any instructions because they felt like an insult to my intelligence, in the sense that they implied I didn't know things—that, and the fact that I'm a lazy bastard.

While we were upstairs, my aunts and uncles and the other people who had been over for dinner the previous day returned to the house. Most of them would be leaving on Monday morning to go back to wherever they came from. I wasn't really sure where, although two of them were from Boston. I think they were married. Strangely enough, by the time Steven and I got back downstairs, the relatives were in the process of saying their goodbyes and getting ready to leave the house again. Apparently hours had passed while Steven and I were fiddling with the computer. When I mentioned this to him, he grinned and said that time goes by real fast when you're doing things you like. I was astounded by this insight, and decided to steal it for one of my novels.

Just before I said goodbye to my sisters and their husbands and kids, Steven came up to me and said, "If you need any help getting hooked up to the World Wide Web, Uncle Brendan, you can call me on the telephone and I'll explain how to do it."

"Okay, Steven, when I decide to do that you will be the first person I get in touch with," I said, and it wasn't a lie, even though there was not a word of truth in it. How about that—another Christmas miracle.

After everyone left, Maw came out of the kitchen drying her hands on a damp towel, so I knew that the brunch dishes were done. I looked away in embarrassment. What had come over me the previous day? What had made me think I could stop women from doing dishes? My only excuse was that I possessed so little experience with doing things that I simply did not understand the significance of "activity" to other people. But I have tried to change. It has taken an enormous attitude adjustment. I still don't understand golf, but I am now willing to live with it in peaceful coexistence.

So there we were, Gavin, myself, and Maw, alone in the ol' homestead at last. The dishes were done, the house was tidy, and the rooms were silent. It might as well have been June.

"Thanks for the spy book, kid," Gavin said as we sat down on chairs in the living room.

I gritted my teeth. I had been hoping he wouldn't bring that up.

"I know what you're thinking, Murph," he said.

I noticed that he had excised the quotation marks.

"You're thinking that the disparity between the monetary value of our gifts puts you in a bad light," he said.

Good grief. Was he turning evil again? Was he sticking it to me?

"But as far as I know, Murph, you never had a lick of sense when it came to money," he said. "I understand that, to you, a novel is a priceless thing, and that its value cannot be measured in dollars. I know that in your mind a RamBlaster 4000 is nothing compared to *Kremlin Bloodbath*. So I just want you to know that I feel ashamed that I was not able give you as fine a gift as you have given to me."

Sweet Jaysus. Had Gavin gotten into the muscatel again? He was starting to make me feel melancholy, but in a bad way. He talked better than I wrote.

"I've given this a lot of thought, Murph me boy," he said. "And I have decided to read the spy novel on the plane back to California instead of watching the in-flight movie."

I nearly broke down in tears. Instead I suggested we go to Duffy's Pub for an early nightcap. "I'm buying," I said, perhaps for the first time in my life.

"Ya talked me into it, kid," he said. I turned to me ol' Mither.

"How's for it, Maw? Care to join us at Duffy's for a snort?"

"No thank yeh, boy-o," she said. "Me two hooligans deserve a night out on the town without yer tired old maw cadging dimes for the jukebox."

"Aw Maw, you always paid us back."

"Off with the two of yeh then," she said, flapping the dishrag at us. "I plan to spend a quiet evening at home watching *White Christmas*, *It's Wonderful Life*, *Holiday Inn*, *The Bell's of St. Mary's*, and *Going My Way*."

I sighed. "You always were The Iron Lady, Maw. Do you need a cigar? I have an extra."

Gavin chuckled. "You missed the unwrapping, kid. I bought Maw a Dutch Master corona for Christmas." Such a son.

Such a brother.

He had one-upped me again! Would the cycle never cease? Only if one of us surrendered, I decided. I was surprised that this had never occurred to me before, given the fact that I had honed surrender to an art form. Too bad Scribner's doesn't publish surrender.

We waited until Bing Crosby came on the TV. Gavin put his coat on, but I talked him into watching the part in *White Christmas* where the stone wall collapses onto Danny Kaye during WWII. That's my favorite scene.

Just before we headed out for the evening, I fired up my Bic and lit Maw's annual cigar for her. We left Maw seated in her favorite easy chair, puffing on the Dutch Master and watching Danny Kaye trying to talk Der Bingle into teaming up as a lounge act. I wanted to wait around to watch Rosemary Clooney and Vera-Ellen sing the show-stopping "Sisters," but Happy Hour was starting at Duffy's.

"Lord help the mis-ter ..." I sang shrilly as we drove away from the house, but Gavin told me to clam up. I understood. He wasn't much of an Irving Berlin fan.

Duffy's Pub was the only business establishment open on Douglas Avenue. Festive light bulbs had been strung around the saloon windows, framing the flickering beer signs. They cast a red and green glow on the footprints in the snow leading up to the front door. I noted that none of the footprints led away from the door. It was beautiful.

We stepped inside. The joint was packed. It seemed like everybody in Wichita who had no relatives had gathered in Duffy's to celebrate their good fortune. It reminded me of the Christmases I had celebrated in Cleveland and Philadelphia and Kansas City and all the other cities across America where I had no relatives. I felt like I had come home.

"There they are!" Duffy hollered when he saw us walk in. He drew two beers and handed them to us, then waved off my attempt to pay. "First beer's on the house," Duffy said. "Merry Christmas, boys." My plan worked. Gavin would be required by the rules of etiquette to buy the second round.

All the booths and barstools were filled. There was no place to sit down. Gavin and I had to stand against a wall and sip our beers among all the other standing patrons who were crowded into the room. But I kind of liked it. It felt like we were "roughing it." Then I started to wonder if the police would cite Duffy for a violation of fire-safety codes due to the overcrowding. Standing up while drinking beer was unusual for me, and every time I do something unusual I think of cops.

Then I heard the voice of Danny Kaye. I looked at the TV above the bar, which was normally tuned to sports programs. I couldn't believe it. *White Christmas* was on. I would get to see Rosy and Vera after all. This was turning out to be the best Christmas ever!

I got so excited that I accidentally ordered another round for the two of us and ended up having to pay. But it was worth it. By then Danny and Bing were decked out in dresses and singing "Sisters," while John Law searched the nightclub for them. I love suspense movies.

Of course Alfred Hitchcock was the master of the Hollywood musical. That scene in *The Man Who Knew Too Much* where Doris Day belts out "Que Sera, Sera" is a real heart-stopping toe-tapper. But the granddaddy of all action/adventure suspense thrillers has got to be *The Sound of Music*. Man, I never thought the von Trapp family would escape the Nazis.

After we finished the second round of beers I started to order a third round, but Gavin stopped me. He said he would pay. This is one of the problems I have with generosity. I try to avoid it whenever possible, but sometimes it gets a grip on me and I don't have the willpower to stop being charming. When I was a student at KAU, I spent an entire semester being affable. I quit going to classes, and subsequently my grades slipped. I was on the verge of flunking out when my advisor called me in one morning and gave me a stern lecture. He said if I didn't buckle down, I might get suspended. "How do you expect to earn a living if you don't have a degree in English?"

"I dunno," I said sullenly. I wasn't in very good shape that morning. I had been up all night being congenial.

Then he informed me that I had been put on probation by the dean of the Arts and Humanities Department. But that wasn't what turned me around. I discovered that if the VA found out I was delightful, they might cut off my GI Bill benefits and I would be forced to get a job.

Determined to avoid work, I started acting cranky until the day I dropped out of KAU. It coincided with Mary Margaret Flaherty's refusal to marry me. But after I arrived in Atlanta I dropped my phony facade and started acting like a pleasant chap again. I didn't care anymore. I was headed down the road to camaraderie, which has caused me a lot of problems over the years. For instance, I don't know how many times I vowed that I would never get involved in the personal lives of my taxi fares, but I always ended up trying to help them with their problems. The reason I bring this up is because Gavin nudged me as I was trying to order a fourth beer. It really irritates me when people interrupt me while I'm being magnanimous. I turned on him with a savage glare. He was pointing toward the back of the room. I looked around and saw Jimmy Callahan seated in a booth with three strangers.

"Isn't that your pal?" Gavin said.

"He's no pal of mine," I muttered.

"That's not what I heard."

"What did *you* hear?" I said sarcastically, as I tried to treat him to another round.

"Duffy told me you were sitting back there last night trying to talk Jimmy out of getting a job."

I started to say, "Duffy has a big goddamned mouth," but Duffy came over and asked if we needed a refill.

"Sure!" I chirped.

He filled our glasses at the spigot and set them on the bar. I handed him a fiver and said, "Keep the change!"

After he walked away, I turned to Gavin and scowled, "When the hell did Duffy say that to you?"

"A couple of minutes ago when you were singing along with Rosemary Clooney."

"Oh."

"Why don't you go over and wish Jimmy Callahan a Merry Christmas?" Gavin said.

I shook my head no. I had taken The Final Vow and I intended to stick to it.

"Who are those guys with him?" Gavin said.

"I dunno," I said sullenly. They looked employed to me. They were wearing suits. Even Jimmy was wearing a suit, the kind of suit you see on male models in magazine ads. Suddenly I started to feel uneasy.

I turned to Duffy. He was wiping down the bar where a patron filled with Yuletide joy had knocked over a jar of pig's feet.

"Excuse me, Duffy," I said. "Can you tell me what Jimmy Callahan is drinking tonight?"

Duffy peered toward the booth. He frowned and shook his head. "He's been swilling coffee ever since he got here. The whole lot of them are on the joe."

Fer the luvva Christ.

I turned and watched Jimmy chatting amiably with his so-called "friends." They looked like salesmen to me, although it was hard to tell because they were sitting down. Salesmen never sit down. They always come at you from every direction.

I sipped my beer and tried to imagine Jimmy selling things. I imagined his mind being filled with wild tales about commissions. Oh yeah. I knew all about commissions. "The amount you earn is entirely up to you!" That's what the classified ads say anyway.

I could feel the steel claw of altruism closing around my heart, and suddenly I knew I would be breaking The Final Vow. I shuddered with horror. But then I started thinking about The Final Vow. What kind of a vow was that anyway? One day before the celebration of the birth of Jesus I had taken a vow to stop helping the downtrodden. That seemed sort of backward.

I stood there sipping at my beer, looking at Jimmy Callahan, and trying to follow the thread of logic that had led me to take the vow in the first place. But even as I did it, I knew what I was really doing. I was playing a mind-game with myself, trying to find an excuse to worm out of the vow. I do this quite often. After I've established the parameters of a vow, a pledge, an oath, or any other form of troth, I start examining it like a shyster for defects in logic—particularly linguistic, grammatical, or syntactical flaws that might be incorporated to invalidate the concept. But I always pretend I'm doing it merely as an intellectual exercise, like solving the *New York Times* crossword puzzle.

It worked.

One minute later I was standing beside Jimmy's booth and peering at the coffee cup in his hand.

"You got a job, didn't you Jimmy?" I snarled.

CHAPTER 23

"Who's this clown?" one of the suits said, looking up at me from the booth. He slowly clenched a fist.

Jimmy set the coffee cup down, reached across the table and took hold of his friend's wrist.

"Easy, Todd," Jimmy said softly. "He's a cab driver."

Todd backed off. He unclenched his fist and picked up a pretzel. There was a wicker basket full of pretzels on the table, and not a beer in sight.

"No Murph, I didn't get a job … not yet," Jimmy said. "But I'm going to put in an application tomorrow. These fellows work at …"

"I don't want to hear it," I said. "I tried to help you, Jimmy, but you wouldn't listen to someone who knows what he's talking about. Did you think I was trying to steer you wrong? Cab drivers know how to steer, Jimmy. We're pros. I didn't want to see you take a wrong turn down the scenic route of life, but I guess some people just can't be helped, even when they didn't ask for it."

"Hey fella …" one of the suits said, but Jimmy raised his hand for silence.

I glanced at the guy, then looked back at Jimmy.

"Well Jimmy, you go right ahead and throw your life away hawking encyclopedias or whatever your friends here pound the pavement to unload on unsuspecting housewives. And who knows? Maybe someday when your feet are covered with blisters, a kindly cabbie will take pity on you like I tried to do and offer you a free ride because you didn't earn enough commission for a one-way ticket home. So Merry Christmas, Jimmy. I gotta go."

"Hey guy ..." another of the suits said, but Jimmy intervened again. It was probably a good thing he kept intervening. I was so miffed at having someone ignore my advice that I was losing my perspective. These guys were fairly large. I thought perhaps they were Soloflex salesmen. I really ought to buy a Soloflex. That ThighMaster was a bust.

Jimmy leaned toward the middle of the table and started talking quietly to them. The suits leaned in and gave him a listen, then they sat back and looked up at me. They started grinning. Not the broad grin you see on, for instance, Jimmy Cagney's mug in a movie just before he K.O.'s a punk, but rather the small, wise grin you see on Humphrey Bogart's face when he catches onto something that amuses him in a dark and ironic way, the sort of grin that lifts one corner of his mouth just far enough to let you know that he's as mean as he looks but isn't all bad.

"So you're Murph, huh?" the guy named Todd said.

"What's it to you, pal?" I said. I could feel my fists aching to curl. That's usually the sign that I'm in the wrong place at the right time.

"Nothing," he replied. "Except that Jimmy here told us about you."

"Oh yeah?" I said to fill some dead air while I collected my thoughts. "Oh yeah" is a much better thought collector than "Uh" when you're faced with impending violence.

"Yeah," he said. He still had the Bogie grin on his phiz.

I looked at the other men seated with Jimmy. They all had the Bogie grin. I made a quick calculation and concluded that this might turn out to be the worst Christmas in the entire history of the Catholic Church.

"We've all heard about *you,* Murph," another suit said.

By the way, I hope you're not annoyed at me for constantly referring to these guys as "suits," but that's how Anita Loos referred to studio bosses in Hollywood, and I always liked it.

"We first heard about you from Yellow Cab," Todd said.

Something funny must have been happening on the surface of my face because the trio started chuckling. As you might have surmised by now, I'm fairly used to people chuckling at me, laughing at me, and even guffawing at me, but for some reason this incident rubbed me the wrong way. Normally I join in on the laughter. I really do need some kind of goddamn therapy.

"Saaay, what is this?" I said, looking from one face to another.

"You're Murph the taxi driver from Denver, Colorado," Todd said.

I started to get goose bumps. He sounded like a cop. I decided to be honest. Cops do that to me.

"I don't understand," I said. "What are you getting at?"

Jimmy and his buddies glanced at each other, then Todd said, "You're the Rocky Mountain Taxicab driver who brought that murdered girl back from Hollywood and took practically every hack in Denver to the cleaners."

"First of all, she was not murdered," I said. "I brought her back alive for crying out loud. And second, I didn't actually bring her back myself, she came back on her own."

"Sure she did," Todd said, giving me a sly wink.

"What's the hell's going on here, Jimmy?" I demanded.

Jimmy was grinning big. He pointed at the three suits. "Murph, I want you to meet Todd, Biff, and Vinny. They drive for Jayhawker Taxicab right here in Wichita."

I looked from one man to another, only this time my jaw was

hanging wide open. To my knowledge, this was the second time in my life my jaw did that. The first time involved a draft notice.

"Have a seat, Murph," Jimmy said, "and let me explain."

Todd and Biff squeezed over, and I slid into the booth next to them. Jimmy took a sip of coffee and set the cup down. "I decided to go ahead and take your advice, Murph," he said. "I drove down to Jayhawker this afternoon to put in an application to be a cab driver, only the employment office was closed because it's Christmas day. I forgot about that."

I was impressed by his obliviousness. Jimmy had the makings of a true asphalt warrior. The Italian Stallion said it best in *Rocky*: "To you it's Thanksgiving, to me it's Thursday."

"So while I was standing around in the on-call room wondering what to do next, these three fellows came in," Jimmy continued. "They had just finished their holiday shifts, and we got to talking. I told them what you said about cab driving, and to my surprise they told me they had heard about you through the grapevine."

"Everybody knows about you, Murph," Vinny said. "You bankrupted half the drivers in North America. You're a living legend."

"I won't be a living anything if word gets out that I'm in Wichita," I said.

"You can say that again," Biff said. "As soon as Jimmy told us he was your friend, we hustled him out of the on-call room."

I didn't know whether it was Jimmy's Christmas surprise or the three beers I had drunk, but my mind was reeling. There was only one thing to do: have another beer.

"Can I stand you guys to a brew?" I said.

"Maybe next time," Vinny said, "if there is a next time. Tonight we're drinking coffee. We gotta keep our heads clear."

"Why is that?" I said, signaling to Duffy and sighing with relief. Any way you sliced it, coffee costs less than beer.

"We're cramming," Biff said. "Tomorrow morning we're taking Jimmy down to Jayhawker and getting him set up. He has to take some tests and we're going to make sure he knows the answers."

"Are you helping him cheat?" I said, withholding judgment until my back was to the wall as usual.

"Worse. We're helping him study," Biff said. He reached into a pocket of his coat and pulled out a map. I knew it was a map even before he started unfolding it. Asphalt warriors can spot maps and billfolds a mile away.

"This is a map of Wichita and the surrounding metro area," Biff said, spreading it out on the table.

We used coffee cups and the beer mug that Duffy handed me to hold the paper down. It was kind of thrilling in a nostalgic way. It reminded me of college, except the ratio of coffee cups to beer mugs was the reverse in college. There was always one troublemaker who drank coffee while cramming so he could actually absorb information and ace the test, the kind of guy who wrecked the curve for everybody else.

Biff tapped at a spot on the map. "Airport," he said, looking at Jimmy. "All roads lead to the airport. Don't ever forget that."

"Say Murph," Todd said. "We heard that Denver got a new airport awhile back. DIA. How did that work out for you cabbies?"

"Not so good," I said, shaking my head. "You make great money going out there, but the waiting time for a trip back can run anywhere from three to five hours."

"Eeeuuu," the Jayhawkers said in unison.

Then they leaned into the map and started showing Jimmy the

locations of public buildings and business establishments that he would be questioned about when he sat down at the cab company in the morning and took the test. Museums, sports arenas, malls, prisons, jails, holding cells, any place where people go and don't have cars to get there. They pointed out the quick routes, the shortcuts, the busy streets and the long red lights. They were trying to do for Jimmy what they would have wanted someone to do for them when they were newbies—transfer all of their knowledge of cab driving from their brains to his, like in the episode of *Gilligan's Island* where a mad scientist transferred Gilligan's brain to Ginger, and Mr. Howell's brain to Mary Ann, and the Professor's brain to Mrs. Howell and so on. The one thing I didn't understand though was why their voices were transferred, too. It seemed to me that their vocal chords would not be affected by a process that involved the shifting of brain-wave patterns from one person to another through electronic helmets. But then I was an English major in college. I didn't take any classes in physics or screenwriting.

As I watched the Jayhawkers work on Jimmy, I began to feel sort of left out because when it came to the economic landscape of Wichita I didn't have much to contribute to his education. But then the conversation turned toward the more refined aspects of taxi driving, such as the best method of increasing the size of a tip, or how to remove unsightly stains from a backseat, the sorts of things that most cabbies pick up on the job. I was brought into the conversation then, and it turned out that I had seven years more experience on the road than either Biff, Todd, or Vinny, so they deferred to my judgment when it came to the nuances of tossing out drunks or stealing fares from Yellow drivers at the mall.

Yet I felt uneasy about all this. Ever since I had entered first grade I was opposed to the idea of studying in general, and cramming for tests in particular, because to me, studying is like cheating. I mean, what's the point of taking a test if you already know the answers? As far as I'm concerned, it's the people who don't know the answers who need to be tested. That's why I never studied. I wanted to know exactly what I knew. The fact that I blew all my tests confirmed my theory. But at least I didn't delude myself into thinking I knew anything. Let's admit it. If everybody who got an A on a test took the same test three months later without studying, they would get the grades I got, which ranged from D+ to D-. As far as I'm concerned, I'm the only honest student who ever lived.

But I did understand. After all, I was a professional cab driver and I knew that if Jimmy Callahan was going to pass the taxi test, he had to come up with correct answers. There was just no way around it. Trust me, I know. Of course this has always been the problem with becoming anything. You name it: doctor, engineer, submarine captain, these guys have to actually know how to do things if they expect to get paid. This is equally true of writing. If I actually knew how to write novels I would probably get paid, too. What more proof do you need?

"Can I ask you guys a question?" I said, during a break for a round of coffee.

"Shoot," Biff said.

"Why are all of you wearing suits?"

"I wore my suit down to Jayhawker Taxi to apply for the job," Jimmy said, his face turning red. "I didn't think a taxi company would hire me if I showed up wearing blue jeans."

Even I joined in on the laughter.

"It's a good thing they weren't taking applications today," Biff said. "They would have tossed you out."

"We advised Jimmy to wear blue jeans and a flannel shirt when he shows up tomorrow morning," Vinny said.

I raised a hand. "I may be out of line here, but might I suggest that Jimmy go with a T-shirt?"

"Excellent suggestion," Vinny said. The others murmured their approval.

"But how about the rest of you guys?" I said. "Why the suits?"

"Jimmy invited us to go with him to four o'clock Mass at Blessed Virgin Catholic Church this afternoon."

"You're Catholics?" I said.

They nodded.

"Irish-Catholic?" I said.

"I'm Italian-Catholic," Vinny said.

But of course.

Biff and Todd were German-Catholic.

"Did you guys graduate from BVH?" I said.

"Nah," Todd said. "We graduated from St. Ignatius."

"Wow, St. Ignatius, our old rival," I said. "Your football team clobbered us four years running."

"Make that twenty years running," Todd said. We all had a good laugh over that. What the hell. Even though I had never played football, I did go to the games. It was either that or do homework. So I felt I owed a debt of gratitude to the St. Ignatius varsity football team. Getting clobbered on a regular basis prepared me for adulthood.

"After Mass I went up to Monsignor O'Leary and took The Pledge," Jimmy said. "My friends here stood witness for me."

Whoa.

The Pledge.

"On the wagon, huh?" I said. "Good for you, Jimmy."

"Thanks. Well. You know. I figure cab driving and drinking don't mix. It's not like being a Santa Claus."

His witnesses murmured their assent. I remained mute.

"Nice suit, Callahan." I looked up.

Gavin was standing next to the booth holding a cup of coffee.

"Well, well, if it isn't the Three Horsemen of the Ignatius Loyolas," Gavin said, nodding at Vinny, Biff, and Todd.

"Well, well, if it isn't Gavin Murphy," Todd said. "My older brother Charley told me that you *almost* led the Blessed Virgins to a victory over the Loyolas during your senior year homecoming game."

That was a pretty risky thing to say to an upperclassman, especially one holding a cup of hot coffee. But Gavin just grinned. "How is Charley anyway?" he said. "Still on probation?"

"One year to go," Todd said.

Gavin tapped his wristwatch. "I'm ready to head home, Murph."

I nodded in agreement. The turmoil of Christmas was coming to an end at last. I had done all I could in Wichita. I had broken the biggest vow of my life, helped a man to avoid work forever, and abandoned my plan to destroy my brother. It was time to get back to Denver.

I drained the dregs from the bottom of my cup, then stood up and shook hands with Jimmy, Todd, Biff, and Vinny.

"See you on the asphalt," I said with a wink.

When Gavin and I got home, Maw was snoring in the easy chair. Her cigar butt was jammed into the bottom of a coffee cup. It would have made a nice photo for a Christmas card, but Maw woke up before we could get a camera.

"Ach," she grumbled. "Once again I failed to make it all the way through *It's A Wonderful Life*. How does that movie end anyway?"

"It doesn't," Gavin said, beating me by a fraction of a second.

CHAPTER 24

Checkout time at the downtown Holiday was eleven a.m., so I stayed away until two p.m. figuring to miss my sisters and their families as they loaded up their rental cars and headed for the airport. I had been paying fifty dollars a day for a room I never used. On top of that, the desk clerk made me pay another fifty for checking out late on the last day, so I ended up spending two hundred bucks just to avoid my relatives. The miracles would never cease.

On the flight back to Denver, I worried about the RamBlaster 4000 in the baggage hold. I was certain it would be crushed beyond repair. No such luck. When I arrived at DIA, I caught a Rocky Cab rather than a Yellow Cab for the ride back to my crow's nest. After my conversation with the Three Horsemen, I just didn't feel safe around non-Rocky drivers who had made the tactical error of getting lured into a wager where I was a deciding factor in the outcome.

I didn't recognize the Rocky driver. He was a newbie. Normally when I ride in a taxi, I pretend I'm not a cabbie. I badger the driver with all sorts of moronic questions about cab driving, but I never do this to a fragile newbie. I normally do it to the old pros from the other companies. I like to hear the hooey they tell me about all the money they earn. It's like watching a predictable yet entertaining vaudeville act.

When we arrived at my apartment, I told the driver to pull around back to the dirt parking lot so I could unload the computer boxes near the fire escape. I noted that my Chevy was still parked there. It usually gets stolen when I go away for more than two days.

I carted the boxes up to my crow's nest and put them in a corner. I'll admit it. I didn't set up the RamBlaster right away. This was a massive change in my life, i.e., I had a new thing in my apartment and I was barely used to its existence, much less its presence. On top of that, I was leery of trying to write a novel on a machine—an electric machine, I mean. Specifically, a computer. I did once own an electric typewriter, but I got rid of it because it made me uneasy to know that I wouldn't be able to write unless I was within ten feet of an electrical outlet. Ironically I was always within ten feet of an outlet when I used my manual Smith Corona, but it just wasn't the same. I got rid of the electric typewriter because the knowledge that I had to rely on electricity to write a novel muddled my concentration, so you can imagine what the RamBlaster 4000 did to my peace of mind.

There was another thing, too. From what I had read about computers versus typewriters in a magazine article, computers made it too easy to write novels, and I was afraid of going down that road. Sure I wanted money, but I didn't want easy money. I had my pride. The article was kind of cynical though. It was titled "Even A Chimp Could Do It." It was accompanied by a picture of a monkey sitting at a computer. The article was written by an English professor—"on a portable Remington with keys that sometimes *stick*," he bragged. He said that the permanence of ink saturating typing paper made a writer think a lot harder about what he was going to say than if he merely tapped a keyboard and saw letters made out of light appearing on a monitor.

I skimmed the article hoping the professor would explain exactly how you thought harder at a typewriter than at a computer. But he didn't go into that, which was too bad because I really wanted to pick up some tips on thinking hard.

So as you can see, I had a lot of psychological ticks to overcome before I could start writing with the computer. I felt like I was poised to dive into a river filled with piranha. A friend of mine in college owned a piranha that he kept in an aquarium. It was the moodiest fish I ever saw.

After I got the boxes stacked up, I turned on the TV and cooked a hamburger even though I wasn't especially hungry, but I wanted things to get back to normal, wanted to scrub the residue of Wichita away—not that I have anything against Wichita, but I always want things to get back to normal after I do things. This is one of the reasons I never do things—they cause me to do more things, like scrub.

I carried my burger into the living room and turned on the TV and started channel surfing. Normally I go straight to *Gilligan's Island* when I eat dinner, but since I was "scrubbing" I decided to run the gamut. I like to say hello to all the channels after I've been away for a while. You never know when the cable company will slip a new channel into the lineup. They do that sometimes. I nearly fainted the first time I stumbled across Bravo.

While I was surfing though, I kept looking at the stacked boxes. Even though the computer and the peripherals were inside the boxes, I felt like they were glaring at me and waiting for me to take them out, like a living ventriloquist-dummy locked inside a steamer trunk in a *Twilight Zone* episode. My steamer trunk might have had something to do with that. Every time I look at the steamer trunk I can almost hear my unpublished manuscripts begging me to take them out and rewrite them. In spite of my altruism though, that's one cry for help I ignore.

I ran across a couple of Clint movies while I was surfing—cop shows as well as westerns. *Dirty Harry, A Fistful of Dollars*—i.e., the man with no name. That made me think up a title for a thriller: *The Cop With No Name.* This excited me, but I got over it. The ratio of titles to my finished manuscripts is somewhere in the neighborhood of 5,000 to 1, so I'm used to not pursuing ideas based on titles.

But watching Clint got me to thinking about Western novels. Since I was currently residing in Colorado, I thought maybe I ought to write a Western. There was one small problem though. I had never read a Western, and I rarely watched Western movies, with the exception of Clint. Ergo, it might turn out embarrassing to write a Western. What if someone found out I was trying to write a novel on a subject I knew nothing about? It's true that I don't know anything about female vampires, but who does? After all, they're not real. Unfortunately, cowboys are real.

So there I was, not one minute into a potential concept for a novel and already I was setting into motion the first step in the traditional process of talking myself out of writing it.

I finally decided that, rather than talk myself out of writing a Western, I should just *pretend* I was not going to write one, and then secretly go ahead and write it. The fact that nobody would know I was doing it did not dissuade me from doing it secretly. To be frank, it always takes the motivation out of me when people know what I'm secretly doing.

But since I knew nothing about horses or Stetsons or Abilene, I figured I would have to make something up. In the many creative writing classes I took in college, the teachers told us that making things up was part of what they called "the fiction writing process." So I figured I had an edge because in real life I sometimes made things up, especially in front of judges.

As a consequence, I did something that I had never done before as a writer. I tried to envision what it would be like to ride the high country on a palomino. That didn't work, so I started thinking about gunslingers. Right away it occurred to me that you never see gunslingers anymore. I had never seen a gunslinger swagger into Sweeney's. Then I started thinking how peculiar it would be to see a Denver policeman square-off like Matt Dillon at high noon in the middle of Colfax Avenue with a gunslinger who would say things like, "Make yore move, Officer Bloomgarten." But that didn't seem very realistic to me. It seemed more like something that wouldn't happen rather than something that would happen. This is true of most of my thoughts.

On top of that, I was afraid that if I went ahead and wrote a Western, I would be dipping into the realm of what my creative writing teachers called "formula fiction." I hated the idea of becoming a formula fiction writer. What if I got the formula wrong? Think of how embarrassing it would be if I tried to become a formula fiction writer and found out I didn't have the talent to sink that low?

Then something occurred to me.

I just might be able to find an algebraic formula that would solve my problem.

With that in mind, I stopped writing for the night.

On December 27th I went to the Denver Public Library to do some literary research. I spent a couple of hours in the engineering, mathematics, and physics departments trying to find an algebraic formula for writing novels, but I came up empty-handed.

I finally went to a librarian and tried to describe what I was looking for. However, I didn't want her to actually know what I was looking for because I was afraid that if she learned that there was an algebraic formula for writing novels, The Word would get out and every librarian in town would start cranking out bestsellers. I'll be honest. I just plain did not want the competition.

Consequently, as I was trying to explain to her what I was looking for, I kept leaving certain words out of my sentences, hoping she would just sort of catch on to what I was saying without realizing what I was saying.

I was walking a tightrope.

At one point she excused herself to go get a cup of coffee, and she never came back.

After the library closed, I drove back to my crow's nest feeling like a fool. I knew that if I was going to write a novel I would have to do what I had been doing for the past twenty years: think one up. This did not bode well.

On December 28th, I pulled a taxi shift. The taxi business is always slow during the week between Christmas and the New Year, but this is true of most businesses. As I have said, December 25th is sort of like April 15th, in that Americans give most of their money to someone else at those times of year, so everybody is broke—the difference being that after December 25th everybody seems happy. Don't ask me to explain it. I only explain delusions, and being broke is no delusion.

It was approximately 1:30 in the afternoon on the 28th of December when I stopped at a 7-11 store to pick up a Twinkie. There were no calls on the Rocky radio, and the hotels were dead. I figured the newbies were freaking out, but as an experienced asphalt warrior I didn't need a philosopher to tell me that all things shall pass. I only needed an IRS agent. Every April 15th for the past fourteen years I had paid the exact same amount in income taxes. I could have faxed them a Xerox from last year for all it mattered.

I stopped to browse the paperback rack, and that's when I saw it—a name I mean: *Thomas Malloy.* It rang a bell. I had once known a guy named *Tommy* Malloy in Wichita. Last I heard he had signed a three-book contract with Scribner's for a helluva big advance, and there was talk of a movie deal.

What a funny coincidence, I told myself. I picked up the paperback.

I won't keep you in suspense: it was the suspense novel by Tommy Malloy.

Seeing a published novel written by someone I knew had a peculiar effect on me. It put me into a kind of "trance." I paid for the paperback—I think—and walked out of the store. I climbed into my cab and started driving. I didn't stop until I got to the Brown Palace Hotel, where I parked behind five other cabs.

By then the "trance" had faded away and I saw it for what it really was: reality. But I had so little experience with reality that I hadn't been able to distinguish it from shock. Tommy set me straight.

The first thing I did after I opened his novel was give it an academic critical analysis. I did this by counting the number of words on one page and then multiplying it by the number of pages. It came out to approximately 70,000 words. Then I read the first page and the last page. This had gotten me through seven years of English classes, and it still held true.

Having completed my in-depth study of Tommy's potboiler, I pulled out of the cab line and drove back to the motor, where I turned in 123. I had already earned back my daily lease and gas, but I had not made a dime in profit. This could have been interpreted as an omen, but I preferred to interpret it as the beginning of my writing career.

According to Tommy Malloy's sister, Tommy had made no progress in writing suspense novels until he had bought a computer. So

I decided it was time to get with the program. In this case, the program was called InstaWriter. My nephew Steven had shown me the basics of typing with it, as well as saving files. He said there was a lot more to it than merely typing and saving, but in my particular case he felt I should just do those two things until I had grasped the program better. He looked apologetic when he said this. But I understood. I had seen that same look on the faces of three nuns and one sergeant during my lifetime. The sergeant was due to be discharged after a thirty-year hitch and had given up hope.

After I assembled the RamBlaster in my bedroom, which was the only place that I had extra space for a new piece of furniture, I sat down and turned it on and brought up the InstaWriter program. It made me feel good to know that I wouldn't be burdened by the thinking that always accompanies typewriters. I was now going to be writing with light. Okay. I'll admit it. I was going for the easy money. I was betting my entire career on the prophetic words of an English professor: "Even A Chimp Could Do It."

I felt like I had stumbled across a gold mine.

That got me to thinking about gold mines, palominos, gunslingers, and Abilene.

Need I say more?

Yes, Virginia—I still drive a taxi for a living.

The End

DOCTOR LOVEBEADS

BOOK 5 IN
THE ASPHALT WARRIOR
SERIES

COMING SOON

CHAPTER 1

I was sitting in my taxi at the cabstand outside the Brown Palace Hotel pondering the nature of my latest miscalculation. I was fourth in line, with two cabs parked behind me, and frankly I needed to go to the restroom. But I was leery of leaving my cab for fear that a crowd of fares would come out of the hotel and I would not be present to take any of them to Denver International Airport.

It had been a slow day. It was nearing five in the afternoon, and while I had earned back my seventy-dollar lease payment and the ten dollars worth of gas I had bought at dawn, I still hadn't shown any profits for the day. Ergo, I was afraid to leave my cab for fear of missing out on a decent ride that would put enough money into my pocket to make the day worthwhile. It looked like it was shaping up to be one of those shifts when I would be lucky to take home twenty bucks profit.

Let's cut to the chase. The fear I was experiencing was a form of mental illness known only to cab drivers. Nobody was coming out of the Brown and heading for the airport. I had been sitting at the stand for fifty minutes and the sidewalk was dead. I had sipped two cups of 7-11 joe prior to pulling in, and now I had to activate an emergency Number 1, but I kept thinking that an avalanche of human flesh would spill from the doors while I was down in the classy johns in the Brown Palace. If you've never been inside the men's room at the Brown, you really ought to visit it the next time you're in Denver. Each urinal is bordered by privacy walls made of exquisitely attractive polished brown marble. When you close your eyes you feel like you're in New York City.

Anyway, I put up with my own nonsense for fifty-one minutes, then I climbed out of my cab and entered the Brown and went down to Times Square. I was gone two minutes. When I got back out to the sidewalk there was not a taxicab in sight, except mine—Rocky Mountain Taxicab #123 was alone at the curb. I read the tragic tale the way Natty Bumppo could read the secrets of the woods in up-state New York. An avalanche of human flesh had spilled out of the hotel while I was gone.

Just to confirm my irrefutable conclusion, I walked over to the doorman, William, a black man who had been guarding the palace gates longer than I had been hacking the mean streets of Denver.

"Where did all the taxis go?" I said, falling into the technical jargon employed by born losers.

"DIA," he replied. "It was like a circus out here for two minutes."

I nodded at William. I knew that the odds of another avalanche occurring within the next half-hour were slim to nonexistent, like everything else in my life. I had blown an entire hour in front of a hotel and had not made a dime. Everybody who had ever driven a cab in his life was laughing at me right at that moment because the way you make money in a taxi is by taking calls off the radio, i.e., jumping bells and not loafing in front of hotels or in the cab line out at the airport. You prowl the streets, you keep your ears attuned to the radio and your right hand gripping the microphone ready to pounce on any call. When you sign on for the day, you don't sign on to eat Twinkies and sip joe and read paperbacks. You sign on to hump the asphalt, jump the bells, get the fares in and out of your backseat as fast as possible. That's how a pro puts money into his pocket.

By the way, that isn't me talking. That's a friend of mine named

Big Al, the cabbie who taught me how to hack fourteen years ago. It's the standard speech that he makes at the end of a training day, after putting a student through the wringer. He even has it printed on a sheet of paper that he gives to all the newbies before turning them loose. The sheet costs only a dollar but you have to buy it—that's what he told me anyway.

Here's the funny thing though. It never would have occurred to me to eat Twinkies and sip joe in front of a hotel if Big Al hadn't mentioned it in the first place. I guess there are some things you should never say to people, and I'm one of them.

When I first started driving a taxi I had every intention of working hard. It was like when I got drafted into the army, I had every intention of being a good soldier. But at the end of my first week of basic training I happened to be sitting in the day-room watching television. I saw *Caught in the Draft* starring Bob Hope and my army career went to hell.

I wandered back toward my cab. "Wandered" is the operative word here. I felt like wandering right past it and continuing until I found an easier way than cab driving to earn money. This, of course, is a scientific impossibility. There is no easier way to earn money than driving a taxi, which is what makes it so difficult to bear when you actually do not earn money. Not earning money is virtually impossible in a taxi, and yet somehow I had managed to do it. I felt like someone who had disproved Einstein's Theory of Relativity. A lot of nuclear scientists are going to be loitering in breadlines when that day comes.

"Got any spare change?"

I froze.

Was I talking out loud again?

I recognized the cadence of that sentence. I'll admit it. I once panhandled on the mean streets of Philadelphia. I tried it only one time though, and the pedestrian said no. It made me feel like a fool. I felt like someone who was only pretending to be a panhandler. I assumed the guy said no because he could see right through me and knew I wasn't a hobo. He was right. Truth be known, I was walking to an agency that paid guys like me to pass out handbills, but I tried panhandling because it seemed like a good way to get free money. I'll try anything to get free money. I buy lottery scratch tickets, but let's move on.

"Spare change, mister?"

I finally emerged from my self-pity and looked around. Three hippies were standing on the sidewalk looking at me with entreaty in their eyes. I know entreaty when I see it. I used to employ it when applying for employment.

My heart soared like an eagle, which is hard to pull off when you're bummed out. Wow, I thought to myself, when was the last time I used the term "bummed out"? Probably in college. There were still a few remnants of hippies around back in my college days. I somehow managed to get in on the tail-end of hippiedom. After the army I grew my hair long and went to college on the GI Bill. This was at Kansas Agricultural University (KAU) in Wichita, Kansas, the town where I "grew up." I had failed as a soldier, so I thought I would try my hand at failing as a college student. I succeeded. I tried to fit in with what was then defined as "The Youth Culture." I did this by attempting to talk cool. When all my college buddies were cramming for their finals, I was studying the writings of cultural icons such as Ken Kesey, Timothy Leary, and Frank Zappa, trying to learn the lingo, the diction, the idiom of our nation's troubled youth. I figured the only way to become "in with the in crowd" was to trick them into thinking I was groovy. I'm pretty sure I tricked a couple of them, but they were freshmen.

CPSIA information can be obtained
at www.ICGtesting.com
Printed in the USA
BVHW01s0907271117
501329BV00006B/883/P